Open my Eyes, that I may see marvellous things

Open my Eyes, that I may see marvellous things

Alice Allan

Open my Eyes, that I may see marvellous things

First published in Great Britain in 2017 by Pinter & Martin

ISBN 978-1-78066-390-6

Also available as ebook

A CIP catalogue record for this book is available from the British Library.

Set in Dante

Printed and bound in Malta by Melita Press

This book has been printed on paper that is sourced and harvested from sustainable forests and is FSC accredited.

Pinter & Martin Ltd
6 Effra Parade
London SW2 1PS

www.pinterandmartin.com

For my children, Cara and Sylvie

There is no such thing as a baby,
there is a baby and someone.

D.W. Winnicott

Mariam

The doctors' café of St George's Hospital smells of cinnamon tea and mango juice, coffee and cardamom. The sweet, spicy scents mingle with the earthier smell of the old building. The patients' various odours of poverty and disease don't permeate here.

Chatter and laughter echo off the tiled walls. The sounds are joined by the clinking of cups and the clang of oxygen cylinders being delivered. Sitting here, in my midwife's scrubs, red-brown skin, cap over my braided hair, I fit into the medical crowd. Here, I am camouflaged as I drink my coffee. Surrounded by all these East Africans, I could pass for one of them. But I know better. I am an interloper. Thirty-three years in England makes me more English than Ethiopian.

My birth mother's here, in Ethiopia, somewhere, unless she is already dead, which is highly likely. Everyone said I'd go looking for her. When I went off to do my voluntary service overseas, even my adoptive mum, June, thought she would lose me to another woman, and since Dad died I'm all the family she has. She needn't have worried. I proved them wrong. Call it stubborn, but I just don't see the point of looking. I'm here in Addis Ababa to work and learn; to build up professional experience so I can say that I 'walked the walk'. Anyway, I don't need to find her; I know her quite well enough already.

I see her in the faces of the young women on the ward who turn their gaze away from their newborns. Those women are wet coals, damp wood; with them the radiance, the fire of new motherhood does not catch. Perhaps inside those blank bodies they are screaming as they pack their few belongings, avert their eyes from their mouthing babies and walk away. To the observer they seem cold, indifferent. They are hard to forgive. But the other midwives have sometimes shown me the tokens that the mothers leave behind; small wooden crosses, a plastic flower, a piece of red string. Then I forgive them. My birth mother left me no such memento.

Ah, well. Better drink up. My shift's about to start. I drain my coffee cup to the sweet, gritty dregs.

There are nine flights of dusty, dirt-speckled concrete steps to climb to reach the labour ward. Three flights for every month I've got left in Ethiopia. Of course, I'll be doing pretty much the same job when I get back to the UK, but things are more raw here, there's more at stake, and it hurts to think of leaving. I sigh, pausing on a landing. I'm thirty-six. My work is my life. I've been a midwife so long that most of the time I do it without thinking about it. Capable, tidy, efficient. Good in a crisis, that's me. But just sometimes... that look of shocked wonder when a mother meets her child's eyes for the first time gets me when I least expect it. The new dawn of innocence and all that. I know it's just an illusion. Life's destined to disappoint. But it's an illusion that keeps me going. I keep climbing.

The labour ward is cool, the dingy corridor lit by a flickering fluorescent tube. In the tiny office, I read through the notes of the new admissions to see who's arrived, and then check who's been discharged. Through the glass I scan the patients, putting faces to names. There's a skinny girl in bed three who has a scar that pulls the centre of one eye downwards, like an exaggerated teardrop. Her dark face is closed and unreadable. She must be terrified, poor thing. I can't find her notes, but the head midwife updates me.

"She came in this morning. They found her, collapsed outside the hospital. She's thirty-four weeks' gestation but labour has already started."

"That's early, especially since she's malnourished. The baby will be small."

"We are trying to slow it down. Perhaps with bed rest birth can be delayed. But she may lose the child."

"What's her name?"

"She won't give us her name. She says she's eighteen, but I don't believe it. Look at her... she's so small. She says she's from Merkato but her accent is from the country. She's probably just been sleeping in the market since she got to Addis."

The girl replies to questions monosyllabically, in an almost inaudible mutter, but I already know her story. One of seven or eight siblings, probably, not counting the ones who died in childhood. Her family scrape a living on some hillside, far from any main road. She'll have been taken from school when she was twelve to help at home with the cooking and the younger children, then at fifteen, to avoid a long-arranged marriage to an older man, she'll have run away to Addis, set on becoming a housemaid, with a uniform and a little box room to call her own. But people will have taken her shy country ways for sullenness, wrinkled their noses at the rancid smell of the *kebe* butter she dressed her hair in. She'll have been ruled out of work because she didn't know how to use an iron or a vacuum cleaner. Hungry, she'll have begged in the street, unable to return. One night, maybe for many nights, she'll have taken coins from a man who filled her belly in more ways than one.

The midwife interrogates her.

"Have you been eating well? Did you have any check-ups? You're lucky you're not HIV positive," she says, scanning her blood test results. "Next time use a condom."

The girl turns her face away at the insensitive suggestion. To speak of such things is shameful; besides, men will pay more for not having to wear one and rough up girls who insist.

"The baby is small," says the midwife. "We may not be able to stop it coming."

I pat her arm. We give her steroids to mature the baby's lungs and tell her to rest.

Half an hour later, though, she tries to stand to go to the toilet and her waters break. She begins to contract more strongly and there is no way now to prevent labour.

I wheel her to the delivery room. While we wait for the obstetrician, I put on gloves and ease her stiff legs apart. I move two fingers inside her, feeling for the soft ring of her cervix; she gasps with pain. She is six centimetres dilated. It won't be long before she is ready to deliver.

"Baby is coming," I tell her in my clumsy Amharic. I wish I knew more words so I could comfort her. Instead I make do with rolling her onto her side and massaging her back with the heel of my hand. The minutes pass. The doctor does not come, but soon the baby will.

The pains come close together now; she does not cry out, but writhes, her arms above her head, gripping the bars of the metal bed. I see the beads of sweat on her top lip. Finally, the obstetrician sweeps in, and five students, all men, troop in with her.

I brief the doctor in English. The students look bored by the girl's labouring. Probably they are embarrassed. One checks his mobile, another yawns and looks out of the window at the swaying tops of the cypress trees. The girl closes her eyes, as if she could pretend the shame and pain away. The doctor makes her put her feet onto boards that stick out from the bottom of the bed; she must hoick her knees up to tighten the pressure in her belly and present her private parts for delivery. I hold her hand; with each strong contraction, she grips it tightly.

The doctor examines her again. She tuts loudly.

"When did they cut you?" she scolds, running her gloved thumb over the scarred lump of the girl's excised clitoris. "They shouldn't cut you. It's illegal. It's not allowed any more, do you hear? If you have a female baby and you cut her, you will be taken to prison. Do you understand?"

She whimpers in understanding. I squeeze her arm tight. It was hardly her fault. She was probably only a baby herself.

Another contraction comes, a strong one that transforms her belly into a hard egg. She writhes and hunches, pushing down with her feet onto the boards.

"This baby won't come," says the doctor cursorily. "I will have to cut you. You need an episiotomy."

The young woman nods blankly. As the obstetrician is reaching for her surgical scissors I lay my hand on her shoulder to stop her, smiling, but not with my eyes.

"You don't need to do that," I caution.

She draws herself up, offended, but I hold my ground. Does she not see the irony of this other kind of cutting? She won't add injury to insult on my watch. Her hand hovers over the scissors before moving away.

"You can try to push," she tells the girl.

So the girl strains, grunting. Pauses. Turns to me, round-eyed.

"It hurts," she says, dismayed. Another contraction comes, a strong one, and with just one more push the baby finally slides out of her.

The baby is tiny and blue and female. It is covered in whitish vernix and it doesn't breathe to start with. We work quickly to resuscitate it with a mask and bag. Its flaccid body twitches into life but its breathing is erratic, so it is bundled up in blankets and taken to the intensive care unit for monitoring. I am left with the girl. I would rather they had kept the baby with its mother; given that little scrap a few minutes of pleasure.

After they've washed her down, and taped a precious sanitary pad onto her bare skin to catch the worst of the bleeding (like many of the women I've seen come in, she doesn't own a pair of knickers), she tells me her name. It is T'irunesh. It means 'you are good'. She can't be much more than sixteen. She doesn't ask me how the baby is.

"Does the baby have a father?" I ask her.

She keeps turning her face away as if it will make these questions go away. I suddenly feel exasperated by her.

"You are a mother now. How you are going to look after this baby?" I ask impatiently.

The girl turns to me then with a look of astonishment that makes me shut my mouth with a snap; I see that it has never once occurred to her that she would keep the baby. For a few seconds, I am face-to-face with my mother on the day she had me.

Mariam

Screw serendipity. I'm not letting a chance meeting like that open up old wounds. I've met girls like T'irunesh before. And more unwanted babies that I can count. She caught me off guard, that's all. I'm not going to try to read any sense into it. Her story has nothing to do with mine. Nothing. It wasn't even my choice to come to Ethiopia, only some bureaucratic muck-up. I was down to go to Sierra Leone. I only accepted Addis because I didn't want to make a big thing about it, didn't want people to think I had 'issues' with coming to my birth country. I took on this placement on my own terms. No hidden agenda, no soul-searching, no identity crisis. I set the pace. And the limits. And I'm not going there with the motherless child stuff.

I write up my notes in a fug of irritation. The head midwife has to ask me three times to take some blood samples to the lab before I hear her; I seize the chance to get out of the ward. You can't close circles. There is no grand design.

Climbing the remaining flights of stairs to the top floor of the hospital, past the patients who sleep on the landings on their cardboard mattresses, past the hollow-eyed parents waiting for news, I rise like a freediver from the shady depths, surfacing into the bright light. And I find, as I always do, that a weight lifts from me. The thin air of high altitude makes my heart beat like someone near-drowned, but it is only up here, far above the chaos of Addis Ababa, that I can breathe.

In the courtyards of the hospital below me, blankets and bandages flap in the breeze. Beyond it, the golden glint of the African Union building over flat-topped acacias. All along Roosevelt, multistories rise amid the yellow set squares of cranes. On the main drag, hoardings advertise electronics and airlines, but behind them stretch the shanty towns, mosaics of brown tin roofs like crackled mud. They are the real Addis Ababa, an anarchic scramble of a city, thrown up in haste, often torn down at a whim. The capital always was nomadic, and Addis still has the feel of somewhere not quite settled, of people tumbled together, ready to pack up and leave at a moment's notice, not quite trusting enough to commit.

The three long cold months of rains that the Ethiopians call *keremt* have finished. The mud has dried, but the earth hasn't yet turned to dust. This is mountain springtime – scorch or chill. Step out of the burning sun into shade and you shiver. The city is ringed by peaks; behind me, to the south, Zuqualla, then Mount Fury, rising out of the brown haze, and to the north, the long ridge of Entoto, its sheep-bitten hillsides streaked with golden teff fields, fringed with swaying eucalyptus.

It's been weeks since I found the time to come up here and I'm greedy for these sights and sensations. I stand at the window, gulping them down. These memories will sustain me through the long London winters.

I get a sudden pang of missing Mum. I consider calling her on my mobile, but it's still too early in the UK. I hoped that she would visit me here, but she's had a bad back and can't face the flight. I think the real reason is that it would bring back memories of that other visit, when she and Dad came to collect me. It was a big deal for them. The Red Terror was only just over. Students, even children, had been shot as counter-revolutionaries and left rotting in the street. People were scared, suspicious, hiding behind bureaucracy to avoid recrimination.

She's scared to come alone too, without Dad. The irony of the trouble they went through to conceive, unsuccessfully. The years of medical investigation. The decision to adopt. The decision to adopt abroad. And one year after they got me, Dad went and died from a heart attack. She found him on the kitchen floor, his bowl of cereal splattered across the lino. When people ask, she says she was glad she had a toddler to look after as it meant she had to get on with life. I suppose she always thought there'd be time to fall apart later. She never has though. At least, not that I know of.

Below me, I hear a distant clamour of Amharic, the clanking of a breakfast trolley, the screech of unoiled doors. Someone, somewhere is crying. A woman, or a child. A keening voice like the call of a muezzin. It intrudes on my thoughts. I had hoped for some respite up here.

Out there, above me, wheeling hawks and vultures move silently through the blue sky, catching thermals in the morning air, turning above some slaughter place. From their great distance, they are dispassionate, circumspect; no twist in their guts at the sight of the poverty below.

The crying has grown louder. I turn, and see that the sound belongs to an elderly man. He shuffles to the window near me, staring blindly into the light, wringing his hands, sustaining a high steady keening for his wife, or daughter or whoever it is that has just died. It is the sound of someone for whom grief has cut the thread of life's logic and meaning.

No respite then. I feel the creeping sickness of panic in my gut and throat. In an instant, my professional armour is back. I move decisively and take his cold hands in mine.

"Betam yiqirta, aznallo," I tell him, meeting his pleading gaze directly. I am so sorry, my condolences. But I can't take his pain away with me. I can't carry the weight of his grief, so I squeeze his hands, dropping them before his coldness can get into me.

I leave him, still keening, on the top floor of the hospital. From outside it would look like an act of compassion, but I know better. Life is hard; only hardness allows you to survive it. My compassion is a way to close the door, to pack the grief into a neat parcel that I can leave behind me. To everything its own compartment. It's the only way I know.

I get back to work. Two more babies are born, both healthy. I write up my notes and leave the labour ward to get lunch. But in the corridor, something makes me hesitate, and turn and go to the NICU. Outside the swing doors, peering in, is T'irunesh. She is hunched over, holding her belly. I can't believe they have discharged her yet, though with the shortage of beds it is possible.

"Do you want to see your baby?" I ask.

A look of fear crosses her face. She stifles it. She mimes the gesture for 'phone' and shuffles towards the staircase. So, she is going.

"Wait. Does the baby have a name?"

She looks confused, then shakes her head adamantly. It may not live until tomorrow. The priest has not blessed it. At any rate, it is not alive to her. It will be Baby X, then. Baby X, Merkato.

She is breaking the law by leaving, by abandoning this baby. By rights, I should stop her. Restrain her. Call a ward orderly. But when I see that her leaving is inevitable, something gives inside me. I want her to have the bus fare home, a set of clothes to find work in, the cost of a meal to charge up the reserves of her weakened body. Something that will mean that at least for the next few days she won't have to beg. I slip 200 birr, a fortune to her, into her hand.

"Ameseganallo betam. Anchi t'iru nesh," she whispers. "Thank you very much. You are good."

My mother kept me until I was a year old. T'irunesh has only spent a moment with her child. She shuffles away, easing herself slowly down the stairs, blending into the crowd. I know I will never see her again.

Mariam

The baby is wrapped in a purple blanket, a small bundle with a tube in its arm. Alive. My relief is tempered by its suffering, though. It is tiny, pale, covered in a light down. Its ears are still fused and its eyes are closed against the lights. Its little mouth is making rhythmic sucking motions. It should not have come into this world so soon.

I try not to really see the sick babies; in the same way that I quickly learned to block my nose from the smell of blood and excrement, by breathing though my mouth, I use a different sort of blocked-sight for my medical life. I have to make-believe they are animated diagrams from my textbooks, interesting conundrums to be solved, challenges to be met. Not small people. If I begin to see the blank distress on their tiny pinched faces, the masks of pain, the grimaces, if I let myself fall deep into the despair of the newborn who is seeking his mother, I will be lost.

The baby does not cry. There is seldom any crying on the critical ward. It is not that these babies don't have working lungs, it's that most often they have no one to cry for. Their mothers are sick, elsewhere, dead. At two days old they have learned the futility of crying. These are good, quiet babies, say the nurses, making a lying virtue of a necessity. They don't have time to comfort every screaming infant that is admitted. They have hardened themselves. I don't blame them. I couldn't do the job they do, every day inserting cannulae into tiny veins, watching fever take another tiny life away. Carrying another little body to the morgue. I couldn't do it. All I do is help bring them into the world.

So why do I stop and look at T'irunesh's baby? Its chances of survival are so slim, why do I let this little life lift my spirits? It shouldn't even be alive. Its mother didn't want it. Its father – did he even know about it? It has drawn so little nourishment from the world, arrived too early to take what it needed from its mother, and now it is deprived of her milk and heat.

"Mariam!" calls a loud voice behind me.

T'irunesh's baby starts; although its arms and legs are swaddled I see the Moro reflex, the instinctive startle response, stiffening its limbs. I turn angrily and put my finger to my lips. Sudden shocks can cause brain bleeds or seizures in babies this young. Dr Tadesse raises an eyebrow archly at my insubordination. How dare I, a foreign midwife, chastise him, a senior neonatologist? But I'm not important enough to take too seriously. He grins sardonically and raises his hands in apology.

"Sorry, sorry!" he whispers.

I gesture him outside.

"So, long time I didn't see you!" he exclaims.

I signal a further reduction of volume.

"Sorry, sorry!" He presses a long finger to his pursed lips, indicating his compliance.

He's expansive, tall enough that his white coat rides up and the sleeves of his checked shirt protrude. He has an affronted tilt to his chin and expressive high brows, which give him the look of being enjoyably scandalised. The man's a gossip and he likes a good drama. He's married, but I don't doubt he'd like a foreign girlfriend. A white one would be preferable, but I think he'd settle for me.

"I was just checking on a baby that was born this morning. It's been abandoned by its mother," I say in a low voice.

"Oh, how terrible. These young girls," he croons, stepping closer. "They have no heart. The poor babies. So, shall I get Sister Rahel to call the orphanage and tell them to collect it? You have no number for the mother? No relative?"

"No. No. The baby is prem. Thirty-four weeks, but with a young, malnourished mother, so it's small for dates. The mother is gone. The best thing would be, if it could be kept here until it's term."

Tadesse steps back, one eyebrow raised. Then he frowns, head on one side.

"Well, for a few weeks maybe. But term? That's nearly two months here. We don't have the room."

The words, the request that it stay, came before I really thought them through. A pipe dream, to think they could keep it so long, but now I've said it, I think, why not? Why not compensate for its crappy start in life?

"You have the room," I insist, forcing myself to suggest a hint of flirtation. I place a hand softly on his sleeve. It does the trick. He grins at me.

"You are my queen, Mariam, *negiste nesh*! How can I refuse you? But you must also talk to my *ferenj* colleague Dr Jonathan. He is just back today from England." He pulls me close by the arm, closer than I am comfortable with.

"You've heard why he went to England? His father died. He returned there for the funeral. You know," he whispers conspiratorially, "he told me he was not going to go, that his hospital work was more important, but I said, 'John, John. What is more important than your own father's funeral?'" Tadesse shakes his head in incredulity. "Maybe," he adds,

"Maybe he thought we would not manage without him. But here, see, Mariam," he says, gesturing around the ward, eyes wide with mock astonishment, "despite his fears, all is well." He chuckles at his own cattiness. "I'm going for coffee now. Come and let me buy you coffee. You look tired and there are some hospital matters I need to talk to you about."

Last time he took me for coffee, 'hospital matters' turned out to be a soliloquy about how lonely he was and how his wife didn't understand him.

"Can it wait? I have a lot of work to do. Remember, please don't call the orphanage without consulting with me. I want it here until it's forty weeks."

I am suddenly adamant that the baby should stay. I want to give it some kind of chance; it's fought so hard to live. It needs feeding by tube now, and later careful cup feeding. Human contact to give it the will to survive. I will talk to my friend Rahel, one of the NICU nurses. I will muster my courage and speak to John. I will protect this baby. Somehow.

John

God, am I glad to be back in Ethiopia. This past week someone's had a grip on my guts; the sunlight and the coffee are unclenching my entrails. Even my tiny office on the sixth floor of the hospital feels spacious today. My patient notes are spread out across the table, demanding my attention, but I stretch my arms behind my head and admire the glinting curves of the African Union building. Outside, the sun is shining on Roosevelt, and for once the traffic is moving. I close my eyes and feel the warmth of the sunlight on my closed lids. From this safe distance, I can start to contemplate my trip back to England.

Returning to England is never easy, even without a funeral to go to. It has always been an exile, a place to be endured. If boarding school taught me anything, it was the practice of indifference, towards others and towards myself. A kind of studied numbness that prevented one from feeling anything deeply. My parents believed this to be a positive thing, the kind of toughening up a small British boy needed, the kind I wouldn't learn from a childhood in Africa. I suppose it was good for me in the long run. There's plenty in life to be endured, and you can't be tied to your mother's apron strings for ever. But still, England's a cold damp country, full of cold damp people. I couldn't not go, though. At least it's done now.

I didn't cry at the funeral so I don't suppose I will now. Forty-eight is a bit old for tears. Actually, I don't know if

I *can* cry. My father's death was expected and it changes nothing about the meagre relationship we had with each other. I never felt compelled to visit him in his illness. I'm sure he never expected it. I stopped bothering to keep up appearances long ago. The only reason I went to the funeral was for my little brother. I suppose if it weren't for Barney, there'd be no reason now for me ever to return to England again.

Barney was waiting outside the door of the crematorium. I was the last in; plane delayed and train late. It had been two years since I saw him last. We're both greyer than last time, but it shows more in his dark hair than my blond. He'd put on some serious weight. He looks like a bit of a rugger-bugger, but I know better. There's more to him than that. Seeing him on the step, I felt that familiar, protective surge of regret for him. He should have taught, written books, not gone into law. Still, who am I to say? Violent sport carried him through school fairly unscathed. Unlike me, he's wealthy. Those things count, I suppose.

As I ran up the steps of the crematorium to shake Barney's hand I could almost hear our old man whistling his disapproval from his coffin. He was an old man, always. An old father. Never one for play or games. And despite his long years in Kenya, he never got used to Africans being late for appointments. Always took it personally, even though he knew about the roads, the rains, the transport. Sorry, Father, sorry. I always was more African than you would have liked. As I pulled Barney to my shoulder I caught the scent of aftershave. He used to smell of fruit gums, apples and mud. He gripped my hand and held me away from him in a gesture that was distant, but not unfriendly.

"All right, let's get this over with," he said.

There weren't any of my father's old friends left to send him off. Just some cousins of ours I hardly knew, and the care-manager from the home. A few old ladies, acquaintances of my mother, were still hanging on; I recognised some of them from her funeral by their glinting hawk eyes and their stiffness. Cast from the same mould. They looked put out. When she died, rather rapidly from cancer, a few years ago, I think they regarded her absence from the church flower roster as something of a disgrace, a sort of dereliction of duty. But I wasn't looking at them much, because my eyes were on the coffin.

As a doctor, I know all about the death of the body. It doesn't scare me. I can't bring myself to believe in all that claptrap about eternal life, though I can see why people would want to. Mother clung to it until the last, much good it did her. Death is just the end of your chances to make a go of this mysterious condition called life, and my father stopped trying on that score a long time ago.

They say it's different when it's a family member; I kept waiting to feel something. Part of me wanted to prise open the lid and get one last look at him, but what would that have achieved? It might as well have been a stranger in there.

Barney didn't cry either. He sat looking forward, next to his wife, Emma. There were so few mourners that they'd put us all on the front rows; we were squeezed in together, into one pew. I could feel Emma's warm body plump next to mine; second baby due in a few months and I'd not even met my nephew yet. She smelled fresh. Shiny, dark hair. Her arm was through her husband's and she kept squeezing it. I was glad of her. A new start for what's left of my family. I'd wondered if he would ever find someone, if he'd left it too late. I suppose they must wonder the same about me. God knows, I wonder about me sometimes.

The coffin slid away and I finally felt something: a pain, a stiffness, a seizing up in my chest. A hardening of my heart against a spasm of hurt. All I really had of him were those few short years before I was packed off to school. As his coffin disappeared into the red curtains, as my father was delivered into the hands of strangers, I found myself wondering whether all those years ago, as he drove away from the school gates, he'd felt the same thing and if he'd recognised it as love.

At the wake, held in Barney and Emma's front room, my brother played the host. I sat on the floor with Jake, my two-year-old nephew, and played bricks. He looks like Barney, but he's dark like his mother, with something softer, less defensive that he must get from her. Emma came to chat, heaving herself onto a low chair with a self-conscious grunt.

"I'm so fat."

"Blooming."

"Fat. Like a whale. How are you?" she asked, touching my arm.

"Fine. I'm fine. It's a relief, really."

"Yes. That's what Barney keeps saying. I can't say I really knew your father. But I'm sorry, anyway." Coming from such a close family as hers, she looked mystified by our lack of emotion. My other family, my Ethiopian family in Addis, feel the same. They can't understand my restraint. In their culture, both men and women weep and wail aloud when a relative dies. If we were Ethiopian, Barney and I would have grown beards in mourning. Perhaps they think me hard-hearted.

Emma sighs.

"Barney's not a big one for talking. He's doing the duty thing today. But he misses you. We'd like to visit you in Ethiopia. When the children are older."

"You'd be welcome. That would be lovely. I don't get enough visitors. My housekeeper would be ecstatic."

"No lady in your life then?" she asked. "Ladies, maybe? I'd have thought a handsome bachelor doctor would be quite a catch."

"Handsome. Ha. Hmm. No," I admitted, a bit flattered to be flirted with. "No ladies. Or only sick married ones having babies."

"Well, babies are amazing. You should have one," she grinned, smoothing her stomach and then stroking Jake's hair.

"Yes. But I understand that one needs a lady first. And good ones aren't ten a penny."

"Pooh. The world is full of lovely ladies. Stop being so picky. You're not getting any younger." I should have been offended but she laughed and leaned over and gave me a hug. "It's good to see you, John. I'm sorry it had to be under these circumstances."

The sun was coming up through the cedars when I arrived back home in Addis. The house felt cold. My housekeeper, Sority, had left food on the stove, but it still felt bleak. I should make more of an effort I suppose, decorate or something. The cat, Tibs, greeted me with an accusing *miaow*, leaping onto the kitchen table, butting me with her head and winding her grey tiger-striped body under my armpit. I fed her, made coffee and thought about my brother.

After the wake, Barney never made the time to talk and I came back to Addis knowing there were things I should address, but not knowing how to begin. Perhaps if I wrote him a letter? We always used to write each other letters. Emma might know what to do. Women seem to have a better sense of these things. I showered after the night flight and went into work. After all, where else would I go? Without my work, I make no sense. Love it, loathe it – the hospital is my home. Tomorrow I will go to see Lidet, the woman I call my sister. But she will have questions and concerns that require a brain better slept than mine. She knows me well enough to understand.

Right. Best get on with it then. The office is warm and if I don't watch out I'll get groggy. I yawn loudly and slap my cheeks in an effort to rouse myself. I start reading the patient notes and prepare for the ward round.

A person

He wakes in his ditch to the sound of the mosque. The piece of corrugated iron that covers his hollow keeps the dew off, but though he is wrapped in his woollen *gabi*, the mountain cold has seeped into his bones and it is a few minutes before he can move his joints. He turns his ankles slowly and rubs the round knobs of his knees. Hard stones, hard bones. The blue light of dawn shrouds the shuttered-up souks; pale yellow is beginning to creep from behind the ridge that towers over his hillside. A sweet breeze that promises warmth riffles through the purple tips of the eucalyptus trees.

He rises. Stretches. Greets the day with a smile. Behind the metal compound fences, there are cobbles and low houses with packed mud walls. Women washing, toddling children, dogs that bark. But he does not live inside. Has not done for years. The street is his place now. He knows the warren of cobbled streets, the friendly faces and the surly, the patient, the distantly related, the drunks, the crazies, the fighters. He knows who knows his own story and who doesn't, though he scarcely remembers the details of it any more. He does not mind sleeping outside, apart from during the rains, when the ditch sluices torrents of brown water and he must seek shelter in doorways. He is strong. He has learned to be strong.

Inside the houses all is softness. He tries to conjure it.

The softness of his mother's body, her *shama* draped around him. He was soft then too. Soft clean curls, fat soft legs. Little teeth in pink gums. The soft sad *tizitas* that she sang him, the blurry warmth of sleep. He remembers the feel of the hanging folds of flesh under her arms, the sweet smell of sweat and spice. The first half of his life. So long ago.

When he has pissed and crapped his thin watery stool into the ditch on the other side of the road, he wipes his hands on his greasy trousers. A layer of ingrained dirt coats his oily skin, protection from the elements. He would like a pair of scissors to cut his nails; they grow long like a woman's, but blacker. He opens his sack (*50 kg Wheat, Not to be sold or exchanged*) and sifts through it, deciding on the day's adornment. From among his precious scraps of paper, and the plastic bags he hoards, he selects a pink plastic hairclip, and some pieces of orange raffia he found in a skip. He ties them into his dreadlocked hair. In the palm of his hand he crushes a piece of dirty chalk, mixing it into a paste with his own saliva, and daubs it across his cheekbones. Without a mirror, he cannot see the effect, but it pleases him nonetheless.

He sets out. The soft part of his life is over and he does not grieve it. Leaving it was necessary and it made him a man. A man with a purpose. In his bags, he has his biro and his scraps of paper. He records things. Things that everyone sees, but only he takes note of. Signs that only he can interpret. The words come from bumper stickers, from packaging, from pages of newspapers he finds by the roadside, from his fragmented memory. Alone they are insignificant, but daily, their message is becoming clearer. He thinks about Ethiopia, about his destiny, while he walks his cold bones into life.

Sometimes connections come to him and it is as if a bolt

of lightning has struck him with such force that his feet are rooted to the earth. Sometimes the enormity, the weight of fathoming how things are, how things hang together, is too much. At those times, he stands in the road with the petulant cars honking and hooting around him and bees buzzing in his brain. Sometimes for days he can stare and not see. And then, suddenly, he is himself and walking with direction. He watches his splayed feet in their tattered flip-flops as he strides.

He lingers politely near the bakery. He wishes to be unobtrusive; he wills his feet to make light contact with the ground. He does not like to disturb. The baker's wife, head bent, swathed in white cheesecloth, steps out of the door as she does every morning. She does not acknowledge him. Looking elsewhere, as if to draw attention away from her indiscretion, she thrusts warm rolls wrapped in foil into his hands. He puts out a hand to her in thanks, but she shakes her head. She does not want to touch him. He is unclean. He nods. He always forgets what he has become. He holds the warm package before him, prayer-like, but her duty is done and she has already gone. On holy days, when Christians fast, he will keep her rolls in his pocket until after the hour for lunch has passed. He might be homeless, he might be mad, but he knows what is right.

He walks. On Churchill, the pavements are wide and they have planted jacaranda trees that shed lilac-coloured flowers he sometimes puts in his hair. Down the wide avenue he goes, past stores selling furniture and computer parts. Three lanes of traffic; tiny blue Toyotas and heaving Anbessa buses grunt up the hill. He keeps his head down and breathes minutely to keep out the fumes. Everything he does is measured. When you have to fill a day, you savour each sensation, be it good or bad. Looking for the tiny variations that distinguish one hour from the next.

He walks past the National Theatre, goes down Ras Abebe Aragay, passes under the chill shadow of the concrete pillars of the new railway. There is no shade at Mexico, and the cars and buses grind and beep. It is a relief to reach Roosevelt, to walk under the acacias.

As always, his destination is St George's Hospital. It is the safest place to be if he has one of his fits. Elsewhere in town, the people rush to him and apply their own methods. Once they held him upside down by his ankles until the blood ran hard to his head and gave him blackened eyes for a week. Another time, he woke drenched in holy water surrounded by a crowd of women calling on the Lord. But the first time he had a fit near the hospital, he discovered that people left him alone. Perhaps they think with all the doctors around that it's someone else's problem. That suits him. He doesn't need saving from anything. His fits are not a curse but a blessing.

On the gate a painted saint grapples with a scaly beast. Georgis. George, patron of good things, not least the local beer. He takes his place, wedged into a corner where the shade will collect. It gives him a vantage point, and a hiding place. Not that anyone tries to harm him. Among this crowd he is unremarkable.

He sees the man with the leg twice the size it should be, begging from the crowd. One leg is normal, the other like an elephant's, a great column, puffy but hard-skinned, the trousers split to afford a better view. It is hideous. He must do well from his begging. He supposed at first that the man was saving the money for treatment at the hospital, but now he thinks not. The man is always there, every day. Perhaps if he is cured he will have no income. Perhaps he is incurable. At any rate, God has sent the man his affliction. Surely his role in life is to allow others to buy their piece of heaven through their charity towards him.

He does not quite know what his own role might be, but sometimes inspiration comes to him in marvellous flashes. If only he could remember it afterwards.

Sometimes there is an accident in town and they come running down the street carrying a body between them, dripping dark blood down the pavement. It is another reason why he likes to stay close to the hospital. There is something reassuring about being close to death. It reminds you that you are alive. Especially when you don't have to live with the loss and can move on, thankful that God has kept you for another day. He is not afraid of death. It will come, and when it does the bees that buzz in his brain will die too. It will be good to sleep deeply then.

As the day wears on he looks for familiar faces and thinks his thoughts. The thoughts flit through him; he'd like to catch them, in one of his plastic bags perhaps. His eyes, brown and lustrous, with long lashes, rove as he seeks out his thoughts in the blue sky. Sometimes he catches them on a piece of paper. But mostly, buzzing and piercing, they find a way to burrow out of his head before he can record them. The ones that remain are soft and cloudy; to catch them you would need a special net or maybe a vacuum cleaner. There was an advertisement on a giant television at the crossroads by the National Theatre. It was for a vacuum cleaner. He stood and watched it all morning. The housewife was pretty and her children jumped on the mat in their frilly dresses. He liked that. He likes children.

Sometimes his thoughts are like lead and he cannot carry

them, but has to drag them behind him, muttering. On days like that he doesn't go far from the ditch. He is always turning back. Other days the thoughts trickle through like a sweet stream and he cannot keep from smiling. Then he tries to catch the torrent, to drink it down so he can keep it in his belly. His belly always was less demanding than his mind.

He eats his bread near the hospital, then walks back to the National Theatre to see the big TV advertising music and vodka and airlines and vacuum cleaners. If he can find a spot away from the prowling street dogs, he will sleep in the sun on a grassy intersection, protected by the traffic that grinds past on both sides.

Sometimes a *ferenji* walks up the street. They keep their arms clamped close, their bags slung across their chests. The coffee sellers on their mats don't bother hawking to them; that kind are sniffy about hygiene, they like their cups washed in boiling water and who has the time to heat the washing water? A quick wipe is good enough. Anyway, the coffee's boiled, isn't it? The sunglasses salesmen stalk them, the chewing gum boys and the boys selling wooden sticks for cleaning your teeth tug at their elbows, the other hand prying into their pockets. They are big, these *ferenj*; big-boned, blond, fat, tall, balding, permed, loud, polite and rude, wearing jeans or smart skirts, trainers or high heels. They are all in a hurry. They have to buy some souvenirs from the tourist souks near the big hotels.

He likes to look at the T-shirts in the tourist souk, though when he gets too close the stallholders wave sticks at him. His favourites are the ones which bear the face of the Emperor Tewodros. How he would love one of those T-shirts. The great man glowers, his face proud and fierce, his high Tigrayan hair framing his noble face. Sometimes he stands and raises a slow hand to salute Tewodros before the stallholders shoo him away. When they do, he winds his way back up the hill to his ditch.

The landmarks set off the same thoughts each time. He finds it reassuring. The great gun Sebastopol (its replica anyway) sits in the grass at the roundabout at the top of Churchill. He likes to end his day thinking about the emperor.

They studied him in school; a man of great deeds and great aspirations, the man who made Ethiopia whole. Only Tewodros could bring together the warring tribes, and if they would not be brought, he crushed them without mercy. For this, he deserved recognition and respect. But when he wrote politely to the Queen of England, requesting friendship, and she ignored his letters and slighted him, he grew angry. To teach the English a lesson, he took captives, European missionaries, and made them work for him, making weapons never seen before in Ethiopia. Bigger, better weapons, until finally they made him his greatest canon of all, Sebastopol.

The British came then. He was delighted to receive them. He had the gun taken to his hill top fort at Meqdella and waited for them to arrive.

A great man. A great Ethiopian. The Emperor Tewodros makes him swell with pride. He pauses in front of a shop window, pulling himself up and making a fierce scowl. He peers at his reflection in the dirty pane. It pleases him. His dreadlocks could almost pass for the emperor's Tigray-style braids. He tosses his head, and almost feels the wind on the top of Meqdella, the soft white folds of a fine cotton *gabi* flapping around him. But then he feels shy. He is too young to be a king. Too timid. He tugs at his small beard and rearranges the child's hairclip. The chalk face paint has lasted well. It was a good decision. He wants to stay invisible, but he needs to be seen. This alternating thrust and evaporation of thought dictates his day, his way of life.

As the sun sets he returns to his ditch. He rests his head on his sack, stuffed with its precious scraps of paper. He will find out the meaning of things, and he will make people understand. When at last they do, they will thank him. Perhaps they will let him back inside. It is some comfort that they said Tewodros was mad.

Mariam

Through the glass window of the critical unit I watch Dr John Spencer conduct a ward round. His obligatory gaggle of students hover at a distance. You can see they are scared of him. He has fewer students than the other doctors; I've heard he limits their numbers to reduce the chance of infection.

He's British, but apparently has been in Africa for years. Late forties, at a guess, but wears it well. I was briefly introduced when I arrived, but we've not had reason to speak since. I don't have much to do with critical care. I spend almost of all my time in the labour and postnatal wards. He's got a reputation for being distant, distracted, even short tempered. With his short blond-turning-grey hair and pale blue eyes, he reminds me of a fierce white owl, stalking the corridors looking for students to snap at, blinking irritably in the bright light of day, most comfortable brooding alone on night shifts. The one time I met him, this fellow Brit in Ethiopia, I remember feeling intrigued. We'd exchanged no more than a few words, but he'd spoken quiet, fluent Amharic with my colleague. I couldn't follow what he said, but you could see he was invested in this country, in this hospital. I hoped our paths might cross by chance and I could find out more about him, but my work kept me too busy. I looked for him a few times in the staff canteen, but I rarely saw him there, and when

I did, there was never the right moment to approach him.

Rolling up his sleeves, he prepares himself to examine one of the babies. I see him warming his hands before he touches it. Under the sleeves of his white coat his arms are covered in blond hair. He has the pale, freckled skin of a Northern European, burnt and damaged by the sun. It is hard to imagine a human being less genetically suited to this country; it suggests a certain admirable stubbornness that he has made this place his home.

He lifts his infant patient tenderly, respectfully, supporting its head. His eyes scan its tiny body. After a few moments, he returns it to its crib and, without taking his eyes from it, very gently palpates its stomach. He says a few words to his students, but does not look away from his subject. There is something about the full attention he devotes to the examination that makes me recall the quiet intensity of his conversation on the day we met. Dr John is happier watching and listening than speaking.

Just then, one of the students, a gangly male, not much more than a boy, sneezes. Although the sound is muffled by the glass, I see the student double over, catching his hands to his face. In an instant Dr John has grabbed his arm, and in front of the horrified students, he marches him outside. I duck quickly into the admin office as the door swings open and the student is dragged along the corridor to a distance far enough from the babies to get a serious dressing down.

"Why did you sneeze in there? Are you sick?" Dr John hisses in Amharic.

"I'm sorry, I have a cold," babbles the hapless second year.

"Then how dare you bring your germs into a room full of sick babies?" explodes his teacher in a muted roar. "If you knew you were sick, you should have stayed outside! I won't be responsible for you killing my patients! Now go! Get out of my sight! Go!"

The student scuttles off.

I hold my breath. Eventually, I peek out. Dr John is standing, staring into the critical room, with one exasperated hand gripped tight in his short hair. He clocks me and frowns.

"Ah. Sorry you had to see that. I don't like losing my temper."

"No, no. You had to say something. It's important."

"Yes. Still. You're the new VSO midwife, aren't you?"

"Well, not that new actually, but anyway... Mariam."

"Yes. What can I do for you?"

"Um... could I have a word about one of the babies?"

He looks perplexed. Checks his watch. Then I see him soften.

"Yes, of course. But can it wait? I need to dismiss these students, then I have to see a special patient on the children's ward." He smiles suddenly, as if the whole incident with the student had never happened. "Come and meet him, if you have time. And do tell me, how is your placement going?"

We walk to his tiny office to collect his notes.

"I'm sorry to hear about your father," I say.

"Oh, yes, well. Dr Tadesse told you, did he? My father and I hadn't spoken for years, so, no great love lost there, but these things. Very... final."

"Do you have any other family left in England?"

"A brother. Yes. Barney. Or 'Barns' as he likes to call himself. God!" he grimaces. "So glad it doesn't work with John, that silly thing with the 's'." When he sees I haven't quite understood, he coughs. "You know, Sebastians who become 'Sebs', Ruperts who become 'Rupes'? Doesn't work with John. Fortunately."

I smile at this sudden burst of weird volubility. I wonder if he's slept since his night flight back. Or could it be that he's one of those ex-public school boys who gets flustered because he's talking to a woman?

In the Urology corridor, I breathe quietly through my mouth as we push through the crush of patients. The smell of urine is appalling. There is so much brown: brown skin, brown clothes washed in river water, brown eyes that either look with fixed fear or pain or are focused on the floor; abject waiting on brown corrugated cardboard. I step hurriedly aside as a young man with a bandaged head is rushed down the corridor towards Emergency, supported by two friends. His eyes roll to show us he is still alive, just. We find the staircase and I can breathe through my nose again.

"It's like Merkato," tuts John. "Too many people. They die waiting."

"Dr Tadesse told me you've worked at the hospital for a long time?"

"Yep. Almost as long as the good doctor himself," he says, with a faint trace of sarcasm.

"You came from England?"

"No. Kenya. I came to study respiratory medicine. Towards the end of the Derg and that tyrant Mengistu."

"That must have been a pretty interesting time."

"Well, yes. Of course, the number of respiratory cases rises during the rainy season every year but that year was terrible. There had been a failed harvest. The Derg had Addis in a pretty vice-like grip, which meant curfews, limits on trading and movement. People putting off coming to the hospital until they were really sick. There was an epidemic of pneumonia."

"I don't remember the Derg, fortunately. I was adopted to

the UK when I was two."

"Ah, I see. I guessed you were British, from your accent. But adopted. I see," he says.

He seems unsure how to respond to this personal information. He coughs, and resumes his answer to my question.

"They were interesting times, certainly. In the beginning, when the Russians were sponsoring the Derg, apparently it was easier to get drugs and so forth. But by the time I arrived, the Soviet Union had collapsed and the Derg were on their own. We were really hand to mouth at the hospital."

"How did you manage not to get caught up in all the politics?"

"With difficulty. My colleagues upstairs in Emergency used to mutter about the terrible injuries that some of the students were being admitted with. Cigarette burns. Rapes. Asphyxiation. Injuries sustained during torture inflicted in the police stations and prisons."

"Awful."

"Yes. But it didn't touch us too much in paediatrics, so as much as possible I tried to steer clear. I figured I was more use here, working, than sent back to Kenya. Or in an unmarked grave with a hole in my head."

We arrive at the children's ward, but no sooner do we step through the doors than a father pushes past us with a child in his arms. The child is about eight, pale, bluish-tinged lips, gasping for breath. Quickly, Dr John takes the rigid boy from him and we rush him to an empty metal bed. John shouts for oxygen and gets the mask on his face. The boy's big brown eyes are wide, pupils dilated as he draws lungfuls of oxygen into his suffocating body. John reassures him in fluent Amharic, soothing the boy, instructing him to breathe more steadily and very soon the boy's skin becomes pinker. His father slumps and squats at the bedside, trembling with fatigue, relief and fear. Another few minutes and his son would have been dead.

I hold the child's hand, and stroke the thin tight curls on his bony head while John finds the vein and draws blood. The boy doesn't flinch. Dr John gives the blood sample to a nurse for testing. The father is too weak to rise, but he shows his gratitude by taking our hands and kissing them.

We move towards the next room. I realise I am trembling with adrenaline. I hold up a wobbly hand and Dr John smiles wryly.

"Chances are if it's not TB it'll be one of the medieval respiratory diseases that hit the poor and malnourished. It's always like this in Ethiopia after *keremt*." He stops in the doorway. "Ah! Now, this is the chap I came to see. Hello! How are you feeling today?"

In a barred metal cot is a four-year-old boy with huge eyes and a small top-knot of curly hair. When he sees John, he smiles and flops out a skinny arm.

"This little fellow's name means 'scum'," John tells me quietly while taking the boy's pulse. "Before he was born all his mother's babies died at birth, so she gave him a name that meant that even God would refuse to touch him. He has survived, so far. But he is very sick. You see how his mother has shaved his head in the traditional country way, leaving a tassel of hair at the front? Apparently it's so that if God does decide to take him, he will only have to take the tassel to lift him towards heaven. We're trying to stop God getting him." John sits on the edge of the bed and holds the boy's hand. He chats to him brightly, asking questions. The boy replies weakly, tracing a finger across the doctor's pink palm.

"Damn," John says, skim-reading the notes. "He's on IV antibiotics for a severe chest infection, but they're not having the effect we'd hoped. We need to find one that works for him, and soon. The local pharmacies have got to stop handing out antibiotics like magic sweeties – the diseases are getting resistant to them. Let's just hope we've got something left that'll do the job for my friend Scum here."

He drops his head to the bedside and lets the boy ruffle his grey-blond hair.

"Never fails to win a smile, from even the sickest kids," he grins. "I used to have blond curls. The Angel Raphael, they used to call me. The angel of healing, protector of pregnant women. Hey. Don't laugh."

On the way back to the NICU he asks me, "How are you finding the hospital, Mariam?"

I choose my words carefully.

"Frustrating. Rewarding. Fascinating. Chaotic."

He nods.

"All we can do is react to the chaos we find in life. We can't change the chaos, but there is value in coping, in reacting. I was joking back there. I don't want to be the Angel Raphael. I'm only trying to be human. Aspiring to anything else is a deception."

I stand at his side as he examines T'irunesh's baby with long, delicate fingers. He murmurs to her in Amharic as he touches her. She responds with shivers, stretches, flexing her tiny stick limbs against the cooler air when the blanket is unwrapped.

"Well, she's strong. Her lungs are working surprisingly well. But you know the chances of her developing necrotising enterocolitis or sepsis are high. Especially on formula milk."

"If I could get some breastmilk for her, would you authorise it?" I ask, a thought occurring to me.

"Why would you go to that trouble?" he asks.

I shrug. It's unprofessional to pick out one baby, I know. But sometimes...

He holds me with his blue eyes, assessing my motives.

I smile. He thinks I need a firm hand. We VSO-ers, always going in for short-term thinking.

"It would be a good learning for the nurses," I say. "If she thrives on human milk. I have a friend who can donate. She's had the HIV test. We can do bacteriological screening if you think it's necessary. Also, I would like to try doing some kangaroo care with her, you know, hold her skin-to-skin, to help her growth and so forth."

He raises his eyebrows.

"Around my shifts of course. Nurse Rahel may also be willing and available."

"Hmm," he considers.

"Come on, the baby's been abandoned. No one will kick up a fuss. You know she'll die if she goes on like this. Let's face it, there's a pretty high chance she'll die anyway..." I trail off.

The baby is making sucking motions. Her lips look dry. I need to swab her mouth with breastmilk to get her digestion and her immune response functioning. My best friend, Betty, has a freezer full of milk, I'm sure she'll oblige. She might even drop some off at the hospital this afternoon if I ring her right away.

"Then I leave it to you."

"Thank you," I say, wondering briefly what I have let myself in for.

John runs a hand through his hair and stares at his shoes. What have we forgotten? I riffle through the baby's papers looking for her Apgar score sheet, her blood type.

He coughs.

"Would you like to come to dinner with me?" he says.

The baby

She lies in an open crib, wrapped in a blanket. She knows neither blanket nor crib, only the feel of where they touch her body. She is raw, uncooked, exposed. Burned by the elements. Her eyes are too big for her head. They protrude from her sunken face, milky. She sees shapes, patterns of light and shade, tastes the shadow, feels the bright scent of a probing light like a fiery finger in her sinus. The room is warm, but not as warm as the place she came from; the plush velvet flesh that enveloped her has been replaced by empty air. Any draught that touches her triggers tiny impulses that ricochet within her. Her body is covered in a skin so fine that heat passes through her and her nerves jangle to the slightest breeze. She has no fat. She is not ready. She lives in the moment, caught unawares; each sensation is everything, all consuming. It is agony to be alive and it never ends. She feels noise keenly, feeling with her whole body; it reverberates through her. Her little organs are the drums on which each voice vibrates; the squeak of a door on its hinges is played on her tendons and the unsheathed nerves that run through her body.

The whispering of the midwives is no better. She feels it as a subtle itching, a grating through the veins of her neck, the insides of her elbows; she would like to brush it away, but all her movements are reflexive, unintended, sudden thrusts and jerks. Only the slow, pale wandering of her eyes gives her the sensation of being stationary in her body.

What belongs to her and what is of the world? The world is only what she feels and there is no pleasure in it. A cannula in her arm aches and stings; there is something scratchy on her head, though she cannot distinguish head from hand or heart or heel. She is not whole, differentiated.

She does not rest. In the brief moments when she does not merely live between pain and more pain, she whirrs with hormones that drive her to seek protection, comfort, warmth, breast. That is all she needs. Warmth she has, but without the confines of the womb, the arms, she is nebulous, uncontoured, loose, unformed. Reverberate, reverberate, closer, flex, protest. Falling, falling, forever.

A warm weight on her body. Firm. At first a shock then comforting pressure; she cannot remember, cannot predict. But right now, there is something good. Something sweet at her lips that makes her poke her tongue, unintentional, reflexive. She pushes against the taste, purses her lips. Reverberate. Salivate. The sweet taste again, this time further into her mouth, inside her cheeks, the sweetness oozes in, focusing the whirring chemicals that swill her into a sweet point of loveliness, the first pleasure of her waking, breathing life. Then the warm weighty pressure is released. Reverberation. Protest. Her body is lifted, pain and blood flow, panic and throb of veins, stiff-limbed startle through the air. Reverberation; something enormous, hard, invasive pushed into her face, her breath comes panicked, vocal chords connect to make a small sound, a gag, as a hard, poking pushing object descends through her breathing tube down into soft morass of flesh. Reverberate. Pain diminishing to discomfort. Swaying, moving, warmth. Then she hears it: *der dum der dum der dum*. That sound. It fascinates her, calms her;

she pauses with those seeking eyes; *der dum der dum der dum.* Swaying.

Heat differential. She is moving, from a warm place to a cooler, to a warm again. She feels the pressure change through her transparent skin. The blanket that wrapped her is removed and suddenly her skin, her living skin, is touching something warm and soft, something alive, a someone else whose presence gives her shape. *Der dum der dum der dum.* Her tiny heart beats as fast as a mouse's, but this slow pump reminds her to breathe. She can hear the rush and swoosh of the blood and it sends echoes of recognition through her own frail body; miniature capillaries, tiny lungs relay the sound. She smells something sweet and turns her face to it, mouthing. Reverberation.

On her lips sweetness, a cotton bud dipped in another woman's milk, and through the tube they placed in her nose, warmth, fullness, trickled gently into her stomach. She sucks her tongue, vigorous, ravenous for comfort. The singing nerve on the roof of her mouth releases pleasure, opiate distraction. She knows the bliss of sucking in warm arms; they confine, limit the vast emptiness of unpeopled space. She lives and desires to live if there is more of this in life.

A person

The bees are back. They buzz and sting; he has to swat at his head to dislodge them, send them flying from his ears. The evening light is fading and he is heading home to his storm-drain bed. Poor local women sit by braziers, fanning embers that cook fat ears of yellow corn. Others weave through the crowds carrying flat woven trays of *injera* on their heads. His stomach growls. It is a long time since he ate. He tramps his way up Roosevelt, feeling wronged. Marching up the street on the way back from the hospital, he is staring so hard at the toes that poke from his broken plastic shoes that he doesn't see her.

They collide at speed and his bag of belongings bumps into the gutter. He doesn't see who has struck him, but he smells her – soap, medicine, cotton – and as her hands reach out to steady herself, for a brief second, she grasps one of his forearms. It happens quickly but, just for a second, her bare palm touches his skin and, like fire, it scorches heat up his arm. Immediately she steps back and releases him, but he is frozen, staring at the place where her palm gripped his skin. The bees have stopped buzzing momentarily. He is focused on the tingle in the place where she touched him.

His bag is pushed back into his hands. He stares at her feet. They are wearing trainers with blue laces. Loose brown trousers over slim legs. He feels a touch on his shoulder and he holds his breath. A smooth brown hand with pink nails.

What it is doing there? He jerks his head up and looks quickly at her face. An open face, strong brows, full lips, good teeth. Her eyes are concerned. She has braided hair that gathers in a bun at the back of her neck.

He shuffles backwards.

"I'm sorry, I wasn't looking... Are you all right?" she says in English.

Why is she speaking English? A full, fast flood of memory; the satisfaction of a neat jotter, a row of red tick marks. The feeling of his legs swinging under the too-big chair and the hard, plastic pen making his hand sore. He realises that this train of thought has eaten into real time, and he is standing smiling. She is smiling back.

"I am fine. Are you fine?" he whispers in remembered words. He hears the crackle in his unused voice.

"Ah! You speak English! Yes. I am fine. Are you? Sorry. I was walking too fast, as usual!" she laughs. "OK. Have a good evening. I like your hair, by the way."

He raises a slow hand to finger the plastic clips. Yellow hairclips today. Yellow. Eggs. Sun. Urine. The eyes of drunkards. He watches her as she leaves, sees her swerve suddenly into a baker's shop. He stares at his feet, absorbing their encounter. The tingle is gone, but the bees are subdued. He is about to move on when a small package is pressed into his hands. It is warm and smells of cinnamon. Soft.

"Sorry," she says, apologising for the gift as much as the collision. "What's your name?"

He thinks. Should he exchange the gift of his name for the bun? No. It is too precious.

"I am... I am a *person*," he whispers.

She is surprised.

"OK... Well, I'm Mariam. Nice to meet you," she says.

He raises his hand slowly. When he looks up, she is already halfway down the road. The traffic streams down the hill from Sarbet, the sun hitting windshields with a repetitive ticking flash. She turns at the Kera roundabout and he loses sight of her.

He squeezes the cinnamon-scented rolls she gave him. They are soft, like the sensation when they collided. Woman soft. Slowly he begins to walk.

Sometimes, when he can't sleep for the moonlight or the baying of the dogs, he walks through his city at night. Women line the street near Chechnya. The bars are decked with ropes of lights and his mouth waters at the rosemary and roasted meat smell of *tibs* that wafts out. Every twenty paces a woman is waiting for custom. Not with him, of course. *Whoever loves wisdom makes his father rejoice, but a company of harlots wastes his wealth.* He would not waste his seed on them. And anyway, the thing between his legs is a limp mushroom. Though he is still a young man, he hardly has the urge.

He has seen the cars queuing for the prostitutes on Chechnya; their drivers all wanting to buy a bit of softness, a memory of their mothers. But those girls seem hard to him. He is confused; perhaps when you open their clothes they are soft on the inside, like hard fruits that harbour juicy seeds. Few of them wear Ethiopian clothes; they totter in high heels and tiny dresses, or skin-tight trousers that make their legs look shiny and diseased like those of the beggar outside the hospital.

It's the ones with kids that anger him. They beg in the dark, swarming quickly to the cars that park near the clubs, their babies on their backs. He's heard that those women will do it for a few birr, the price of a meal, shifting the sleeping load on their back to a sister for the time it takes. He would like to swoop down on them like an angry God, smiting them and their customers, driving them out into the dark streets where their babies could sleep in peace.

He stops in the middle of the pavement when he has this thought and still the anger of the smiting is in him. He lets it flood through his dirty soles, through the holes in his shoes. He imagines it gushing out into the gutter. A small girl is watching him from the protection of her mother's skirts. He nods at her and trudges up the hill, back to his ditch.

Mariam. A doctor. A lady doctor. The emperor had a wife who taught him softness. Her name was Tawabach. When she died, along with her, he lost his mind.

Mariam

"What are you thinking, woman? You can't go on a date dressed like that!" Betty rolls her eyes in despair. "Come, let me dress you. Sometimes you are like one of my children, *Mariame*, my Mariam."

It's Friday night. The night of my date. And my best friend Bethlehem is right. I don't really know about dressing up. It's not that I don't like to look nice, but I don't want people to think I care too much about those things, because I really don't. That's why I am at Betty's house. I need her to help me dress and I am hoping some squealy, girly time with my friend will get some of my nerves out.

"Oh, Betty, you know I don't have a clue about clothes. Does it really matter what I wear?"

"Yes! Not everyone is as unjudgemental as you. You should make an effort. You're a beautiful woman, if only you'd act like one!"

"I'm sure John won't notice what I'm wearing anyway. I doubt dressing up's his thing either."

"Don't tell me you don't notice people's clothes, their style?"

"Not really."

"But it's self-expression, right? Don't you want to express your personality with your dress sense?"

"Why would I want to expose myself like that? Life's much safer in my midwife's uniform," I joke. "Seriously though, there is one guy's style I like. That guy from the street I told you about. I mean, not what he wears, but the fact that he just dresses for himself, in whatever makes him feel good. I've seen him outside the hospital every day this week. He waves at me. Last week he had all these yellow hair clips in and some kind of paint all over his face."

"You mean that guy from the street whose privates hang out of holes in his pants?"

"Yeah, well, admittedly that particular look isn't so great. I'll try to find him some old hospital scrubs to wear. But there's something interesting, something special about him. Almost like a character out of some historical fable. What did he say to me? 'I am a person...' I mean, who says that?"

"A crazy man. He's touched," says Betty.

I have a thought that makes me snort with nervous laughter.

"What are you laughing at?" demands Betty, intrigued.

"I was just imagining what I'd do if I turned up tonight and John was wearing face paint and yellow plastic clips in his hair," I giggle.

"You are madder than I thought. Get in the bath and clean yourself. You smell of hospitals," chides my friend.

"So will he!" I shout back along the corridor as I head to the bathroom.

The bath is so full of kids' toys that I have to rummage deep in plastic to make room. I play idly with a wind-up frog as I soak. I used to have a little pot belly in England, which would rise above the foam, soft and womanly. After a few bouts of dysentery and a diet with little meat and few cakes, my belly is flat and girlish, a smooth descent towards the foamy bush of hair. I imagine John's hand, white freckled fingers sliding into the warm water, and I shiver. It's been a long time since a man touched me. Careful, he's a colleague. An older, senior colleague at that. And that might not be his intention. Perhaps he wants to talk shop, hospital politics. A bleakly disappointing thought strikes me; perhaps he's gay. Hard to tell with these public-school types sometimes. Bah. It will be a night out, at least. I like the man, whichever team he plays for.

One of Betty's paintings is on the wall; it's of a slender Ethiopian woman pouring water into a pool. Kind of Klimt-inspired; gold overlay, jewel-coloured flecks of paint. It's beautiful. She runs a gallery, selling her art alongside scarves woven by a women's cooperative. They're popular with rich locals and tourists alike. Her little shop doesn't make as much money as Solomon's construction firm, but she can run it and be a full-time mother to her kids. He's away a lot, building his apartments in the north of the country.

I put on one of Betty's long robes and head out into her bedroom. She is feeding Nati. I sit next to her, our shoulders touching as we watch him drift off. One of his pudgy hands is slowly stroking the side of her breast. His sucking slows and he gives a little hum of satisfaction before releasing the nipple and relaxing into sleep. Betty grins at me and gently carries him to the next room.

"How's *your* baby doing?" she asks.

"Still alive," I tell her. "She's so small. The doctors are amazed her lungs are functioning. Without your milk, I'm not sure she'd still be here."

"Plenty more where that came from. I tell you, with number three you can make a whole lot more than one baby can drink. And all that *gunfo* porridge my mother-in-law feeds me. Believe me, I am a human fountain!"

She looks good. Rounded still with her pregnancy weight,

buxom, womanly. It suits her. She wears heavy silver jewellery around her neck; the kids like to play with it while they are feeding. She's just weaned Elsa who's nearly four. Heran, who is three, was the independent one; she stopped when she was two. Now Nati has taken the place at the breast. My friend Betty looks like one of those pottery fertility goddesses. I get a rush of love for her and wrap her in a hug.

"What's that for? Hey! Don't be sad."

"I'm not sad."

"Good. You're doing good things for that baby. Just don't hurt your heart, *Mariame*. She might die. She's so little. You're doing a lot for her, but you can't make her live if that's what's meant for her."

She lets me go and holds me at arm's length.

"How does Rahel feel about this, what do you call it? Kangaroo care? She's taking turns too?"

"Yeah. We talked about it; she can see it will help the baby. She's seeing it as a professional development exercise. We're both realists. We know the risks. We won't get attached."

"Can't she be kept in an incubator?"

"Huh. You know what they call the incubators? 'Isolettes'. Horrible word. She'd be isolated. And without this human contact, she'd die. I'm sure of it. Needless to say, the other nurses think we're crazy."

"Well, you are. Both of you."

"Yeah. Rahel's staying after her shift. It's way beyond the call of duty. I hope we're not making a mistake."

We sit on the bed, looking into her full-length mirror and curling our bare toes together. It's time for me to be getting ready.

"Jeez, I can't remember how to do this date thing. Not sober, anyhow. Maybe I should get drunk. Alcohol makes things a lot simpler."

"Hmph," grimaces Betty, slapping my thigh. "The less said about some of your drunken choices the better. Now, my lady," she laughs, squeezing my cheeks, "I am going to dress you *so fine* that this man, this highfaluting doctor man, Doctor *Lurve* is going to fall at your feet and worship you."

"I don't even know if I want that. I mean... God, it's been so long."

"Just enjoy it. Doesn't hurt to have a few men crawling at your feet. Now sit yourself still, lady, while I transform you into a *goddess*."

Castelli's is crowded. The long wooden-floored dining room is filled with a big table of diners, cackling and chinking crockery. I peer into the corners of the room looking for smaller tables, but John's not there. Perhaps he's stood me up. I feel daft in my grey silk dress. I covered it with one of Betty's nubbly silk scarves, a lovely dusky pink one. Her silver jewellery clanks at my neck and ears. I feel overdone.

The waiter takes me into a smaller room, for private dining. The whole evening is going to be a lot more intimate than I had predicted. I wonder if this was John's choice, or just the luck of the draw. He's there waiting, reading the menu.

He looks up and frowns when he sees me. Great. Now I feel really stupid. He's wearing a soft blue shirt, a bit worn at the collar. It suits him; it makes the blue of his eyes seem brighter. As I fumble with my shawl, he stands to greet me, and we graze cheeks; three kisses, the standard Ethiopian greeting. Somehow a chair gets between us and we fumble and shuffle trying to move out of its way. I feel his grip on my arm and I laugh, grabbing his arm in return.

"Look at us. Can't take us anywhere," I joke.

He shakes his head and grins.

"Yes, I really should get out of that hospital more often. Pretty soon I won't be fit for the outside world; even the furniture is attacking me."

We study the menu; Italy's brief years of occupation has left a legacy of great Italian food, and amazing macchiatos. My mouth is watering. We order antipasti, seafood pasta, beef medallions.

"It feels wrong, doesn't it?" I say, after the waiter have taken our menus. "Gluttonous."

"Hmm. I know what you mean. But starving yourself won't put food in other people's mouths. Anyway, you look like you need feeding up. Am I allowed to say that? I'm not sure what one is and isn't allowed to say any more. Anyway, what I mean is, you've been working hard. I hear good things about you on the ward."

We talk about work mostly, personalities at the hospital. He speaks sparsely about the senior management, but manages to be utterly scathing. I would have enjoyed a bitch-fest, but he's right to be cagey. We're both guests in this system, though he is more indispensable than me.

"Now, listen," he says suddenly, switching on his senior medic voice, tetchy, matter-of-fact. "I need to give you a bit of professional advice. There's something I need to warn you about, Mariam."

"Warn me?" I stiffen at his change of tone.

"Yes. Now I said I heard good things about your work. I have, from your colleagues. And you know that those are the ones who matter to me. But if you want to carry on working and having free rein you're going to have to play it more carefully with senior management."

"What do you mean?"

"I heard you paid to get the toilets fixed on the labour ward."

"Ah. Well, yes, I did. A temporary fix anyway. They need a complete overhaul. They'd not been flushing properly for months; I mean, they worked, sort of, but they were using buckets to flush them, and when I spoke to that guy in the basement, the fixer guy, he said it was only a small pipe that needed replacing. The budget's been frozen. Look, it was only £200 for parts. I thought—"

"I know, I know. But it's embarrassed the management. Shown the hospital 'wanting'. It's humiliating. The management can't have people thinking the hospital is under-resourced."

"But it is."

"You don't have to tell me that! But don't start thinking that nobody else notices or cares. I know the management well. They're all doctors who've been promoted to management positions. They are caring people with an impossible job to do. Every single department is under-resourced; budgets have been frozen for years. You've seen the laundry women washing the bandages. There's a drug shortage in Oncology, the X-ray machines are mostly broken, everyone's clamouring for more money. Good God, I wouldn't want their job. Look, Mariam, you meant well, but there's an issue of saving face involved. There are ways and means. Next time, come to me. I'll have a word in the right ear, and we'll divert the money quietly. OK?"

"OK." I feel suddenly stupid. A cultural buffoon, when all I was doing was trying to help. Was this why he asked me here, to give me a mild ticking off? To prove that he's more Ethiopian than me? I push my lentils and Parma ham around my plate. I can put on a good sulk when I want to.

"I've offended you," he says.

"No," I pout.

"I wanted to tell you before you heard it directly from Dr Tadesse. Shouting it with a megaphone at you across some critically ill baby probably."

I scowl, then relent and giggle.

"So that's why Tadesse invited me for coffee. He actually did want to discuss 'hospital matters'. He wasn't just trying to chat me up."

John is smiling too. There are tiny freckles on his top lip.

"The head of midwifery says you've done great work. I don't want you to feel disillusioned or put off. But I do want you to be able to... to stay with us."

"Well, I only have three more months to go. How badly can I mess up?" I laugh.

He frowns.

"Only three months. And then?"

"Back to England. Back home."

"Home. Ah, I see. And you've no thought of staying on? Extending your contract?"

"No. It's been a two-year placement. It's been amazing, and I love it here, but I have a career. I'm going back to be head of department at the Whittington. The youngest-ever head, I'll have you know," I tell him, showing off.

He smiles, but he is quiet and thoughtful. He takes a few moments to speak.

"Sorry if my advice sounded condescending. Believe me, I put my foot in it so many times to begin with. This is a proud country."

"Rightly so," I say.

"Amen to that," he toasts, taking a sip of wine. "Let's not talk shop any more. Tell me about yourself."

I tell him about my life back home, and he probes deeper.

"I can't imagine there are many Ethiopians in Gloucester."

"No. I was, well, very visible, shall we say."

"I know a bit about that. No. Hang on. That's not right. I know absolutely nothing about what it is like to be black in a white country. Very different, I'm sure, from being white in Africa," he says, looking flustered. "Not the same at all."

He takes a sip of wine.

"You really don't want to find her, your birth mother?" he asks, uncomfortable to be speaking openly about such a private matter. "Forgive me, it seems strange to me that you came here but haven't looked for her."

Not him too.

"No, I *really* don't," I laugh. "Anyway, I doubt she's still alive. Now tell me about you."

He takes the hint and changes the subject.

"Not much to tell. Born in Britain, grew up in Kenya. Boarding school, Medicine. Came to Ethiopia. Specialised in respiratory disease and then neonatology. Been here ever since."

There's more that he's not telling me.

"What made you stay?" I ask.

He fixes me with those blue eyes. He looks tetchy. Takes a sip of the good Rift Valley wine they keep plying us with. Holds my gaze and raises an eyebrow.

"A woman," he says.

Is he telling me he's married, or is he flirting with me?

"Ahh..."

"Not what you think," he smiles. "She was a girl of

seventeen when I met her. I saved her life. She had TB, was very sick. The doctors had written her off. Sometimes there's one patient who you just can't let go. *You* know what I mean. I've seen your stubbornness with that baby."

"So what did you do?"

"I got her drugs, used my connections. Pulled in favours so that senior consultants saw her. Home visits. I stuck with her until she was fully recovered."

"Why?"

"I don't know," he sighs. Then he decides to trust me. "Well, yes, I do. Her parents were desperate. Like that little boy Scum, she was an only child. She fought it tooth and nail. I don't know. I was in my twenties. Maybe because she was so pretty," he laughs. "But by the time she was better she'd become more like a sister to me. I felt responsible. I couldn't leave. Her family became my family. I realised, one day—" He swills the wine around his glass. "I realised one day they meant as much, maybe more to me than my own family."

"What happened to her?" I ask.

"Hmm?" he responds vaguely. "Oh! Well, nothing happened to her. I mean, well, everything. She's still here. Still pretty. She has two children. Not mine, I hasten to add! They're my godchildren, not that I'm exactly a believer."

"That must be interesting. To live here long term and not believe. Everyone here is so devout."

"Well, I'm afraid I lost my patience with religion after a couple of years in Ethiopia. It made me angry. Religion, in my opinion, can turn people into sheep. I see why they want something to believe in. The human mind creates order from chaos to survive. But this acceptance, no, this *veneration* of suffering... There is no value, nothing admirable about the suffering of the poor. We wealthy, to whom misfortune so rarely comes, kid ourselves that tragedy makes people noble, or that they are raised up through their suffering. It's a lie. There isn't enough anger. People suffer too much, they accept too much. Suffering doesn't ennoble – it's dirty and sad and it destroys the sufferer's capacity for hope and happiness."

"Wow. You sound like you've thought about it a lot."

"Yes. Well, I've had to make my peace with living here. As you have done, no doubt."

"So what's your philosophy then, all things considered?"

"Oh, I don't know. How about 'Eat, drink and be merry, for tomorrow we die'," he jokes, raising a glass.

"'But alas we never do,'" I say. "Who said that?"

"Dorothy Parker."

"Ah, yes. You don't seem very merry," I counter.

"Do I not? No. Not so good at following my own advice."

"What's her name, your Ethiopian sister?"

"Lidet. I have lunch with her and her family every Sunday. She makes a mean *doro wot*."

I laugh and feel a cool rush of nerves. Coffee is coming. And after that? What next? This is dangerous. Despite his obvious nerves and social awkwardness, I really like this man.

After dinner, he drives me back to the door of my compound weaving though the grinning packs of dogs that own the road at this time of night.

"Thank you, I really enjoyed that," I say as he pulls up. The moment of truth. "Um, do you... want to come in for coffee?"

"*More* coffee?" John laughs, then realises his faux pas. "Ah. I – I should get back," he says uncertainly.

Suddenly I feel like a floozy.

"Yes, of course. Early shift tomorrow."

"No. No," he says. He clears his throat. "It's just that, Mariam, I didn't realise you'd be leaving quite so soon. It might not be a good idea to get involved. And I'm not just looking for, well..."

"I see."

"So... perhaps it's better..."

"Right. Only..."

"I know. This life..."

"Yes. Well."

"I'm sorry, I... Good night, Mariam."

He leans over and his cool dry lips briefly brush mine. I shiver. He's probably right, but God I want to kiss him and screw the consequences. We move apart, sensible adults. *This life*... I pull Betty's scarf around me and let myself out of the car. Even after he has driven away I feel my lips burning.

A person

The rubbish collectors wake him. That is what starts it. The feeling of being persecuted. They come with their big metal carts, heaving them between them, coming to empty the overflowing skips in his part of the *kebele*. The street sweeper women call out, in those high girlish voices that make the sound carry through the scarves they wear over their faces. They wear broad-brimmed straw hats and canvas coats to cover their dresses. Their brooms have known unspeakable things found in gutters and ditches, but they are aggressively cheerful today.

He crawls slowly from his ditch like an animal. He had stomach pains in the night, and the white lice that cluster at the band of his trousers and in his armpits bite him mercilessly. He feels more than usually vulnerable to attack. Where are his courtiers? Sometimes, when the shifting time zones of his memory collide and overlie, what's real and what was read, long ago, loop though his head until he cannot distinguish one from the other. Was it only in a book that he read about the emperor? It seemed so real. In that book the emperor took a hostage; that was the moment when the world began to listen, when the world began to take him seriously and, after years of neglect, began to pay him the respect he deserved. He knows it ended badly, but that is not the part of the story he remembers. The part he remembers had dignity in it. Squatting, shitting in his ditch, he craves that dignity above all else. He must get clean. Wash the black filth from his oily skin. He has been meaning to wash for weeks.

He takes himself up to a cobbled lane he knows, away from the tarmacked roads where cars roar and rumble. This lane is only an overgrown thoroughfare for mothers and children on their way to school, mop sellers taking a shortcut, the odd herd of grazing sheep. There is a marshy pool where a leaked pipe has filled a ditch. Lush green grass surrounds the pool.

He undresses methodically, peeling the layers of ripped material from him as if they were silken garments, woven by his artisan weavers. He shakes each one, holding it to the light, considering the seams, inspecting for lice. There are many lice. He pops one between his black fingernails and inspects his own red blood. He dips each layer into the marshy water and rubs it against itself. Then he lays it onto the warming rocks to dry. With each layer, he feels more peaceful, reduced, free. He would like a place to keep his things so he did not have to always carry them on his body. They weigh him down with their inadequacy. They are so pitiful. If he kept them somewhere else, he could remember them in better glory. Instead he is always reminded of how inferior they are.

He is naked. His blackness, the oneness of him, pleases him. He stretches in the sun, feeling free from the pinch of his ill-fitting jeans. He needs new trousers. They are full of holes, especially at the crotch. His balls get cold and shrink inside him when the rains come. A woman and a child pass and he steps aside, turning his eyes to the wall in modesty. She keeps her head down, her face hidden in her *shama*, but her little boy, shaven head, tatty blue school uniform, drags his toddling heels and stares at the naked man.

He steps into the pool. The Emperor Tewodros on his hilltop never had such a bath. It is deep and cool. He sits immersed up to his waist, tall grass surrounding him on all sides. He is invisible to anyone on the path. He leans forward, his head between his knees, dipping his mass of dreadlocks into the water. He feels for the band that holds them up and they release like black water snakes, tumbling into the pool. He flicks them back and sits, examining his nails. He would like soap. The sun warms his chest. He picks at the tiny tuft of hair that grows there, pulling each one out by the roots until his chest is bare. Unclean hair. He rubs his armpits, twirls a long fingernail into each waxy ear.

He feels magnanimous. It was a mistake to feel wronged. Sometimes the world tests our patience and resilience. He must try harder to respect the lives of those around him. There are people who must go about their business, he accepts that. They cannot understand the importance of his role as observer of his people. They cannot know the import of the notes he takes, the plans he draws. If they knew, they would bow low to him. *Yes, all kings shall fall down before him, all nations shall serve him. He will redeem their life from oppression and violence and precious shall be their blood in his sight*. But instead they are misled. They should not prostitute themselves to foreigners, taking their handouts. They should have pride in their country.

No one has ever conquered Ethiopia; only the devious Italians, who due to their chemical bombs squatted here for a while. But they could not contain this vast dry land of mountains and history. In the mountains of Adwa, the village women threw berbere chilli powder into the Italians' eyes, blinding them so their menfolk could slaughter them.

Simple deeds from patriotic people. His chest swells. How proud his people will feel when he tells them what is coming.

He knows, oh, how well he knows, that things thrown on the garbage heap soon all smell alike. Just so the faces of the drunk, the lost, the mad. They all look the same before long. But he is different. He will not enter their ranks because he has a mission to lead by example. He eschews the chewing of khat, doesn't drink *arege* or *tej*, sweet honey wine. He is proud of his virginity. Certainly, he will never have a child. He is for higher things.

The sheep come suddenly from all sides before he has had a chance to see them. Suddenly he is overrun by a ginger-cream herd, pushing and jostling around him, starting and bleating, their furry balls dangling and their fat tails shivering to discover a fresh piece of grazing. They crowd around him so that he cannot stand. He feels woolly flanks pushing against him and he panics. They will trample him under the water. He grabs at the backs of two sheep on either side and tries to haul himself out of the water. The sheep buckle under his weight; one splashes into the pool with him, roiling and stumbling, making the water a mire of mud. The other sheep voids itself in panic, its little pellets floating on the top of the frothing water.

He finds his feet, yelling silent abuse at the sheep as they push on, stupid creatures, fattening themselves on the way to the abattoir. He feels fury rise inside him, but it is not the sheep, but his people who bear the brunt of his fury. Once the Ethiopians were lions, roaring their strength from the flag, lions of Judah, the black-maned lions of Ethiopia. They rose up, embattled, to defend their honour. Now they are fattened, docile. Lambs to the slaughter. He will not join them. Though he be ripped apart, he will stay a lion.

He stands dripping in the shitty water. The stupid woolly smell of sheep clings to him. *By the rivers of Babylon there we sat down. Yea, and we wept when we remembered Zion.* His clothes have been trampled. A band of pressure tightens around his head and he feels the wrongs done to him building up until he cannot contain them anymore. He pulls on his wet dirty clothes and stumbles up the track until he comes to the road. He walks like a blind man into the oncoming traffic. Cars beep and swerve to avoid him as he rails against each oncoming vehicle. He feints them like bulls; roaring his silent displeasure. The world displeases him today; he will have none of it. They come and come, a never-ending stream of insults against him. In his heart, he is gentle, magnanimous; he would walk smiling among the people, but the world wrongs him. He has a little pride only, but when it is piqued he will fight for his place.

The cars slow and form an orderly line, single file. No one is surprised on their morning drive by the raging man in the road. He will make them late for work, but they know how to wait and be late, it does not stress them. He takes care not to touch the cars; his flailing is not intended to damage or destroy, just prove his point. The drivers can see he is desperate; some bless him, some roll up their windows. Most keep their eyes fixed forward, blocking out his pain. Pain is never far beneath the surface of life; the trick of survival is to ignore it, to act as if it wasn't there. Numb yourself. Or things will fall apart.

John

I have died and gone to heaven. Anna is crouching over me, red-haired and tiger-like, tracing her tongue around my nipple. My body is younger, tauter, hairless and we have drunk half a bottle of brandy and the remains of a bottle of absinthe. It is the night that she deflowered me, luring me back after anatomy class, back through the icy fen winds to her cold Cambridge digs and she is undressing me slowly. I am too drunk to move but it feels exquisite, like life is beginning. I am on the dissecting table and she is removing my body parts piece by piece. She whispers in Latin to me as she moves: *gracilis, adductor magnus, pubic symphysis*. I wonder if this is what love feels like, but when I turn to kiss her, she has gone.

Instead it is Selam's lips that meet mine. The rush of love and guilt is painful; her sweet bespectacled face is lifted to mine and her lips are soft and warm. The hospital store cupboard is cramped. Surrounded by blankets and bandages I devour her, knowing we don't have much time before we will both be missed on the ward. I push my hands up through her curls and she grinds herself into me. She is everything and I am lost in her voice, her laugh, her intelligence. I have found my place. I will live out the rest of my days in Addis Ababa with my beautiful Ethiopian doctor wife. Someone is coming; she breaks quickly away, rearranging her white coat. I am breathing so heavily that she laughs and shushes me. She puts her hand on the door handle, bites her lip.

"My flatmate is away this weekend," she promises.

She is gone and I am suddenly scared. I set off searching for her, pacing the halls of the hospital, finding myself back at university. I throw open a door to find Anna, straddling another man. In fury, I fling him from the room and try to grab her but she evaporates, then suddenly she is on top of me, and I know it is the last time, and I realise she never loved me anyway and as I come she hunches over me and bites my shoulder so hard it draws blood. She is gone again, but the bed is littered with the dirty playing cards we used to pore over in my old school dorm; naked women are strewn across the bed; I pick up a card and find each one bears an image of Mariam, eyes scornful, challenging, daring me to look at her naked body. Daring me to make myself vulnerable once more.

I wake, my head fuggy from last night's wine. I have a useless erection. Either I have overslept, or Sority must have come in early, because I can hear her in the kitchen washing plates. With that domestic sound, the women of my past, and my desire, recede. I could have slept with Mariam. She wanted to. God knows I did. But I stopped having one-night stands a long time ago, and if she's really leaving in three months, what's the point?

There's something in her that I recognise. I'm more drawn to her than I thought I would be, and that's dangerous territory. When I asked her out, I kidded myself she might stay longer, that this country had claimed her, the way it did me. But all that's irrelevant now. I'm not a fool to put myself through all that pain again, not when there's so little time. All those years ago, when Selam left me, left Ethiopia, I was like a sleepwalker for months, bereft, betrayed, abandoned.

I've too much to lose for uncertain returns.

Mariam will head back to London and bars and boyfriends and whatever it is young people do in England. She'll settle down and meet a nice man and have his children. My Ethiopian family are praying for me to find a woman. I should never have mentioned to Lidet that I was going on that date. It will only have got their hopes up. At the wake, it felt time to turn over a new leaf. Find the courage to try the field again. I let myself be seduced by Emma's conviction that there is a good woman out there for me. I was stupid to be so naïve. It's not that easy.

Swiftly I pull on shorts and trainers.

Sority, in her yellow headscarf and housecoat, is standing in the kitchen doorway, blocking the morning light with her bulk and her concern. She shakes her head when I tell her I'll eat later, but after all these years, she knows me too well to argue.

I run. My usual loop, up into the hills beyond the French embassy. It is a reassuring pleasure to feel my feet make contact with the ground. I run first over cobbles, past a straggle of houses and shops lined with dusty cedars, then out into the yellow, thistled fields, following the dry donkey tracks that criss-cross the slopes. Smells of wood smoke, berbere, sewage. As I run, I turn inside myself, focusing on the complaints of my body; they remind me that I am alive. You don't cover ground fast at this altitude, it's all about pacing yourself. It's not the legs, but the lungs that you're working. You must manage yourself, know when to be restrained. It's all about doing the distance.

I first saw Mariam in the cafeteria. She thinks she passes for an Ethiopian but I could spot her for a *ferenj* a mile off. The way she holds herself, holding herself in. The Ethiopians are more fluid, there's no sense of space between them. The women, even the female doctors, sit, legs entwined, hands on each other, cheeks touching. But she, like me, can't let herself go. She's nervous, wanting it, fearing it. It marks her out as much as if she were as blond and blue-eyed as I am. I'm surprised they don't shout after her in the street, catcalling, "You, you, you, you! *Ferenj!*" as they do with me. I feel for her. I understand. Perhaps that understanding is what draws me to her.

There was a boy in my year at school, I can't remember his name, who cried every night for the first term. I can picture him now, curled into a tight ball, his back towards me at lights out, sobbing his tiny, tight spasms of shame. He was eight years old, like the rest of us. None of us knew what to say. We were busy managing ourselves, and we had no language to deal with emotions. It was grown-ups who were meant to do all that, but the woman whose job it was to turn the lights out, Margaret, I think her name was, only told him, in her brisk, brushing-away voice, 'Come along now, you'll see your mother in six weeks.' Six weeks. We carried the bleak emptiness of waiting inside us. I used to stare into the dark, listening to him crying, wanting to howl along with him, but knowing it would do no good. You weren't allowed to phone home and even if you could, what good would it do? What difference would it make to say that I was lonely, that I missed Kenya, the houseboys and my friends in the village, that I missed eating *nyama choma*, that I missed the sunshine and the dogs. All that would have to wait for the Christmas holidays. When I think of school, mostly I remember the smell of detergent and the feel of boiled sheets.

The first thing Mother asked me when I returned that Christmas was, "So. Is it all *marvellous*?"

"Yes. It's all wonderful fun. Super," I replied manfully, because even at eight I knew that it was all costing a great deal of money and that it was terribly good for me. Convinced by my enthusiasm perhaps, my parents sent Barney out to join me a year later, as soon as he turned seven. At school, we would make connections that would compensate for all those things we missed in Kenya. We would get on in life. Make something of ourselves. In the second term, they had to drug the boy in the bed opposite to get him to return to school. He stopped crying after that, so I suppose it got easier for him in the end.

Selam, the beautiful doctor I'd let myself imagine a long life in Addis with, left. She took a job in the States, for all her talk of saving her people.

"You come too, John. Come with me. It's only for a couple of years. We can return to Ethiopia afterwards. Bring back what we've learned."

"You know I can't go. I'm needed here. Here. Not in America. And let's not kid ourselves. You won't come back. You're leaving me."

"I'm not leaving you. I *will* come back. I love you. Why are you being like this? I don't want this to be goodbye. But, John, this is a chance for me. A chance to learn, to meet people. A chance for me to make something of myself."

"Fuck you, Selam," I told her, the hard, chosen words a bolt sliding across a door.

I got used to life without her, the same way I got used to life at school. The hospital is an institution, and I know all about those. I learned to manage myself. To keep busy. Action. The myth of progress. There is a lot to be said for the distraction of work. When it comes to pain, the ache is the long-distance runner. At least when I run the ache inside me, the ache of absence, is made tangible. I can massage it away.

I have reached my destination. I mount the ridge and stand, heaving for breath despite my restraint, my hand resting on the rough bark of an acacia for support. The city is a great sprawling shimmer below. The golden façade of a high-class mall in Magenagna glints in the sunlight, piercing the orange haze of pollution. The light railway snakes a path between slums and palaces. Far away, on the horizon near Old Airport, I think I glimpse the tip of the African Union building. I can't see the hospital; it's hidden by trees and other higher buildings, but I can feel it. It's always there. Its need and my duty towards it, the worth it feeds me in return. A black ant crawls over my hand, and when I look I see a trail of them winding from the dusty earth towards the sweet blossoms above. I shake the ant away. A chill breeze dries the sweat on my back, silvering the leaves of the eucalyptus and mimosa. I really should get back. If I stand still, I will stiffen and suffer for it later. It is tempting to race back down, leaping over hummocks, giving in to the elation of gravity, but if I stumble I will fall, and the rocks here are sharp razors of obsidian. I cannot afford to get hurt. I stretch, feeling the morning sun briefly warm my pale exposed belly, then at a slow, careful jog I pick my way down.

Mariam

I went on a bender. That's what you call it, isn't it? When you drink so much that time bends and warps and you can't remember if the last time you slept was two or three days ago, and if the tongue in your mouth is your own or someone else's. That's what I did. I can't remember what the impetus for it was – perhaps just that gradual feeling of accretion that I get, like a build-up on the lenses of your glasses, when the world outside seems to get misty and further away. When you feel like you're walking through life buffered and fuddled and numbed and – nothing touches you. The edges of things get blurred. And that's before the booze.

The booze made things real; like a warm light coming on in my gut, the blood ran faster. I could talk to people again, get that sentimental feeling of connection that only comes with being pissed. I loved the warm relief of alcohol, the way you could draw a line under what happened the night before and blame it on the booze. The way it erased yesterday. And then there's the element of unpredictability. Things happened when I drank. Mostly sex happened.

I moved from nursing to midwifery because I didn't mind the unsociable hours and I was pretty sure I'd never want a family of my own. Too complicated, given my background. Never something I could imagine happening. At nursing college, there were a few men, smuggled back into halls, or sharing my single bed in my grimy lodgings. White boys and black boys. I never wanted much more than that one night though. They were usually gone before morning. After all the anatomy lectures, the all-female environment and the careful touch involved in clinical practice I enjoyed their roughness, the deep rumble of a male voice, the smell of them, beery and sweaty and warm in my bed. I expect they left happy. Maybe I used them. So? Men use women that like all the time. I don't know if I hurt the feelings of the men I slept with. I didn't think about it. One of them told me I was a 'hard bitch' and it pleased me. Who wants to be soft?

But that bender. It scared me.

I wanted to sleep, but he wanted sex and I couldn't be bothered to argue. Through my half-open eyes, I hardly knew what he looked like, much less knew his name. He was a bloke I'd picked up in the bar a few days ago and we'd been drinking and screwing fairly consistently since then. A proper British bender. I didn't know where I was. Not my bedroom certainly. He was thrusting against me and it hurt. Not enough to care, but it hurt. I'd drunk nothing but vodka for nearly three days. I knew I was going to get cystitis, that as soon I was sober I'd be off to the GPs for antibiotics. I turned my face. I didn't want to look at him. The pillow smelled bad; salt and mould. I just wanted to sleep, but he kept pounding. Somewhere in my brain was the niggling fact that I had to work on Monday. Was it Saturday or Sunday today? I didn't like him. I'd had only fancied him, and now I never wanted to see him again. His thrusts had pushed me up the bed until my head began to bang against the headboard. *Smack, smack*. And suddenly I was three years old again.

For a couple of years after the orphanage, when I first came to the UK, I used to bang my head on things. I remember the sensation. It blocked out everything else. It was painful, but effective. Immediate. It moved the vague pervasive discomfort to sharp and self-directed pain. Sometimes I used to get bright lights behind my eyes when I smacked my head against the plaster wall. Behind the lights my birth mother's face was hiding. I knew my mum, my adoptive mum, would come running when she heard the banging so I had to do it quickly and with force. Sometimes the lights were like a door opening and a deluge of forgotten images would tumble through before the next bang slammed the door. My own real bedroom door would burst open and Mum would rush in and lift me to her, hushing and soothing and rubbing my bruised forehead. I'm sure she thought I was doing it for the cuddle. I wasn't, though that was a bonus. I was doing it to forget and to remember. Above all, I wanted to remember my Ethiopian mother's face.

When my head started hitting the headboard in that guy's stinking flat, I sobered up right away and I wanted him off me, but he hadn't finished and he was stronger than I was. I writhed and bucked but he didn't care what I wanted. All I could do was shriek abuse at him, pummel and scratch him as his thrusts smacked me against the headboard. He came, then went off to shower leaving me curled up and sobbing. That was two years ago. I haven't had sex since. Mostly because I stopped drinking with the sole aim of getting drunk. That is, until last night. That's why I'm so pissed off. I'm angry at how raw I feel. At how easy it is to floor me.

My head throbs. My tongue is fat. My face feels glued together, lumpen. My eyes won't open, but I can't sleep for feeling angry. On top of the bottle of red wine I drank with John, I downed pretty much a whole bottle by myself when I got back to my house. Sat on the sofa chugging

Awash Merlot, watching crappy *eskista* videos of women in cheesecloth dresses dancing in windswept fields. The wine numbed the embarrassment of his rejection, but brought on the self-pity. Pathetic. I need to sleep, but I am too angry with myself.

The sounds of the city begin at 5.30 with the call of the muezzin from the local mosque. A little later the Orthodox church starts up in competition, hailing its worshippers from loudspeakers. The low rumble of traffic increases until by 6 a.m., when the red-eyed pigeon that has been scrabbling about on the tin roof joins in with a throaty burble, I am fully awake and furious, with myself, with John, with everything.

I stumble into the shower and lather myself. The steam will make my hair frizz, but I don't care. There's no one to look good for. Even though his rejection was honourable, flattering even, it is still a rejection. A 'no thanks, I'd rather not get into a relationship with you'. Does it matter that his reason seemed to be that he liked me too much to start something that would finish so soon? The end result is the same – we are not going to touch. Not going to kiss. Not going to look into each other's eyes. Not going to share the delicious journey of discovering each other. Am I angry because against my better judgement I wanted to get into something, something that perhaps might give me a reason to stay in Ethiopia a bit longer?

Maybe if he'd come back for coffee I'd be waking now with morning breath, fumbling awkwardly for pants and bra, or feeling across a damp bed to find out if he'd done an early runner. Perhaps we'd have had bad sex; maybe we wouldn't 'click', he wouldn't be able to do it, or he'd come too soon, and I'd have had to avoid ward rounds for the next few months. Or perhaps we would have sat up talking, kissed a bit and fallen asleep in each other's arms. I didn't know how much I needed holding until the prospect of being held was withdrawn.

I'm off work today, but I'll go in later to see the baby. She needs to be held. Needs it with a physical compunction that leaves mine in the shade. She hasn't got a name. I've blocked out what will happen when she reaches term. It's only a few weeks away. She's still so small. But, touch wood, she's had no infections and her lungs are getting stronger. There's a big chance her development will be affected long term, but that won't be clear really until she's at least two. Where will I be when she's two? If she survives, and I pray to all the gods that I'm not sure I believe in that she will, I will never know how her story ends. It feels bittersweet. In my mind, I realise I am already leaving this country.

Dressing in my room I hear that Seble has arrived and is washing up in the kitchen. She comes in the mornings to clean and cook. She's Oromo, heavy-set, in her fifties, with hennaed hair, a thick chinstrap tattoo and crude crosses on the backs of hands puffy with arthritis and washing up. She is the most religious woman I have ever met; when she's not working, or babysitting her grandchildren, she virtually lives at the church. She wants to take me on a pilgrimage before I go, to pray for the children I may still have if I hurry up and get on with it. She is concerned I am getting too old. She is a wonderful cook.

She raises an eyebrow when she sees me. I feel like her child today. Her face is mild, concerned. I have embarrassed her, and this is more shameful to me than any judgement she might pass. No doubt she's tidied up the empty bottle and the mascara-covered tissues. But, in this weird intimacy that we have, she will never mention it. For ages, out of shyness,

I used to wash my own knickers, but now she does it. She probably knows my monthly cycle better than I do.

We greet each other in the long formulaic greetings that Amharic demands. 'How are you? How's your family? How's work? Praise be to God. Praise be to God. Praise be to God.' While my breakfast eggs are frying, she chops aubergine and courgettes for one of her famous moussakas. The smell of frying garlic is challenging, but a cup of strong coffee and a couple of paracetamol help. Usually I try to coax her into conversation. It's good Amharic practice and I enjoy watching her taciturn face stifle the giggles when I mix up words. Two years in Addis and I know hundreds of obscure words, *umbilical cord*, *nipple*, *cockroach* and *constipation*, but I don't kid myself. When I string them together, it brings my listeners nothing more than joy and confusion. Last week I asked Seble to boil some cats for supper, the word for cats and potatoes being similar. *Deneuch, demeut*. I still can't remember which is which. Today though I want to stay in my head and mull. After my eggs and toast I return to my room. The sun has come out and it begins to lift my gloom.

There's a picture of Mum on the mantelpiece. It's an old one, from when I was a teenager. She's sitting on the end of my bed, lips pressed together in a tight smile, grey bob getting in her eyes. She used to tiptoe in while I was studying, silently placing a cup of milk and a biscuit on my desk. Then she'd sit on the end of my bed and watch me work. People used to assume from my grades that she was a hothouse mother. Quite the opposite. She worried about me overdoing it. She still does. She's always told me I work too hard. It's true. I do. Like her, perhaps I need not to have the time to fall apart.

I'd like my mother to know the Ethiopia I know. Perhaps

one day we'll come back here together. She had no time to see the beauty of this country when they came to adopt me, to know Ethiopians' warmth, to understand their humour. According to her it was all bureaucracy and uncertainty, stomach bugs and waiting. I feel tetchy that Mum and I are apart, but tetchier at the thought of all the explanations she'll need to understand anything about my time here. Another three hours before I can call her. I hate the time difference.

There's another photo on the mantelpiece of me and Betty. We're in traditional dress – it was taken last Meskel, the day the rains ended. White muslin with gold embroidery. It suits her with her curves. I look like I'm in a costume. Pretending to be Ethiopian. I suppose it's a fair cop. I tease her for being a dippy-hippy, but really she keeps me sane; I could talk to her today. She's so busy though, with the kids and Solomon's work keeping him away from home, with the business. I'll save up my complaints for her until after kids' teatime when she puts a DVD on and is free for a gripe. Right, Mariam, I tell myself. No sulking. Get out of bed and get out into the sun.

I put on tracksuit bottoms and a T-shirt and trainers, let myself out of the compound gate and head out into the street. Seble needs vegetables and I need to clear my head. I walk down the hill to my favourite fruit-and-veg shop. A drover is herding his sheep up the verge. A country boy, woollen throw over his shoulder, shorts tied up with string. His dusty short-cropped hair is reddish from some kind of deficiency, and he is blank-faced with the concentration it takes to keep thirty hungry sheep on the move. I stand as the bleating crowd mills around me, and put my hand out to touch their hard, furry skulls. The boy cracks his whip and the sheep stumble on.

The traffic is constant. I have to keep stepping onto the verge to let the big white Prados with the NGO stickers pass. I shouldn't tar them all, but the dailies that the UN consultants earn make me sick.

There's an old homeless man sleeping by the side of the road under a dirty sack, his greased leather face looking Neolithic, like the Tollund man. For a while that homeless guy near the hospital and I used to wave and nod at each other. I liked his face. Liked his style. His otherworldliness. I haven't seen him for a week now. I hope he's OK.

I step out of the sun into a shadow and feel the mountain chill. Sudden fevers, road accidents. Such things happen. More likely if you are destitute. When the nameless poor die, a black municipal van collects their bodies from the side of the street and they are taken to a cemetery, a mass grave on the edge of Addis. I step back into the sun and shake off my gloom. I'm just hung over. He's probably fine.

Dawit and Ashenafi run the vegetable shop. They greet me with smiles before I take a look at what they've got in stock today. They are brothers. Dawit is the brains. He's older, sociable, speaks some English. He's got bright, inquisitive eyes and has a line in funky T-shirts. Today's says *Baby, it's time*. You could get philosophical about those slogans. I bet he lies awake wondering what they mean. Ashenafi is the handsome one. Under his unsloganed T-shirt, his chest is slim but muscular from hefting fruit boxes. He's about nineteen, with a close-shaven head, and eyes that seem almost lined with kohl. He has the surly look of a man who knows he is beautiful, but either through circumstance or shyness, does not know how to capitalise on the fact. His scowl says he knows, as he works every day in the sun selling fruit, that his own stunning looks will one day wither like an unsold mango. Not that there are many unsold mangoes, judging by the steady stream of shop girls that pop in to buy a kilo or two so they can stand and watch him and sigh. Among middle-aged Addis ladies, and I qualify as one of those in Ethiopia, he's a bit of a local celebrity; Betty is known to pop in for some tomatoes when Solomon's away and she needs a little visual pick-me-up. He's way too young for me, but he's so handsome that I feel a little dazzled. I make myself giggle by imagining myself starting a suggestive conversation with him about cucumbers and melons.

I buy ruby grapefruit, a bag of spinach, fat heads of broccoli, strawberries, mangoes and guavas. When I went back last Christmas, people asked me if there was enough food. I should take a picture of Dawit's heaving stall. Ashenafi tots up the amount and flashes me a quick smile that makes me blush despite myself.

I walk slowly back. I'm so busy with my thoughts I don't see him until he's standing right in front of me. It's the man from outside the hospital.

"Hi!" I greet him, overly enthusiastic, relieved he's avoided the tragic fate I had imagined for him. I see he has lost a shoe. He's unbelievably dirty, like he's been rolling in mud, or worse. I really must get him some old trousers from the store cupboard. I don't usually pick up waifs and strays. Best not get too close to mental illness. One old pair of scrubs won't hurt though.

He blocks my path and I can't tell if he's seen me. There are other people around and I feel safe, but he's got the look of someone with a mission today.

"Good morning," he says sweetly.

"How are you today?" I ask, breathing through my mouth against his smell.

"I am fine. Please take this pen and write," he says, offering me a grimy biro and a scrap of paper.

"Oh, OK. What should I write?" I ask, putting down my bags of fruit and taking the pen and paper.

"G.E.O.R.G. ..." he begins.

"Is that your name? Giorgis?" I ask.

He frowns. Scowls. I have interrupted his train of thought and this seems to cause him consternation.

"G.E.O.R.G.E. B.U.S.H.," he spells out. "I like George Bush *very* much," he says and as his face opens into a broad smile I see that he really does.

"George Bush?" I almost laugh. The ex-president? I went on a march against the Iraq war. In my world, the man is a figure of ridicule, but this guy's clearly been inspired by him. His eyes are shining and it seems for a moment that the mist has cleared. It almost makes me want to like George Bush too.

He's crazier than I thought. I don't know what to do with this situation. It's too weird.

"George Bush," he repeats, reverently.

"OK," I acknowledge. It takes all sorts. "Why do you like George Bush?"

"He is a *real* man," he says.

Out of the corner of my eyes, I see a movement. Two lanky young policemen, clearly convinced the guy is harassing me, are striding towards us. The police are twitchy at the best of times, but recently, with all the demonstrations, they've been more nervous than usual. They approach from behind him, one with his baton raised. The guy hasn't clocked them yet. I put out my hands in a gesture of appeasement.

"*Hulu selam new*!" Everything is OK!

Except that suddenly everything is now not OK, because

the homeless guy, feeling the policeman's baton poke him in the ribs, spins round with a speed that shocks both me and the young officers. His body tenses, up come his hands like claws and his lips curl back to bare his teeth. His face is twisted with affront and rage and he begins to make the most horrible, strangulated noise. It's a sort of hissing, spitting snarl, the noise of a cornered animal or a mad dog. He begins to feint the policeman who poked him with the baton, stamping with one foot, snatching towards his face with his nails, daring him to touch him again with his bubbling, hissing growl.

The first policemen steps back, his face aghast, but the other, now provoked, raises his baton in earnest. He is about to bring it down when I shout out.

"*Beka*!" I tell him. Stop!

I get in front of the hissing homeless man with my arms out, defending him from the police. It's risky. The police can be heavy-handed, gung-ho, and I don't know what the homeless man's capable of. Nothing I'd seen before led to me to think he could react so violently. I don't know if this is a mad act, or the real thing, but I won't see him beaten on my behalf.

There is a moment of stalemate. The policeman and I face each other down. Then, thank God, he backs off. Testily, he lowers his baton. He waves it about a bit, in warning to the still-hissing homeless guy. He waves it at me too, a telling-off for fraternising with a low-life and wasting his time. He tries to look nonchalant as he joins his colleague, but as they walk away I see them muttering and casting back looks.

I turn then to the homeless guy. He is still tense, panting a little, and his hands are still up and still clawed. He has spittle around his mouth, in his wispy beard.

"Are you OK?" I ask, motioning his hands down, exaggerating inhaling deeply to breathe him back to calm.

It takes a few moments, but something shifts. He clicks back into focus. It's as if he has woken having sleepwalked and cannot remember where he is.

"Yes. I am fine. Are you fine?" he asks politely, as if the incident had never happened.

I am still holding his precious scrap of paper in one hand. The one bearing the name of his hero, George Bush. I proffer it to him, my hand shaking a little. He takes it shyly. As we part ways, he waves it at me absent-mindedly, then shuffles off.

I carry my bags home feeling shocked and uneasy. Outside my house an old man sits on the verge, rhythmically pulling live cockerels from a sack. One after the other they appear, like bunches of flowers pulled from a magician's sleeve. The cockerels find their feet and ruffle their indignant feathers; in the sunlight, they shine red, gold and green, the colours of the Ethiopian flag. I want to talk to someone about the incident with the police, the madman who loves George Bush and the beauty of the cockerels. Someone who might understand. Of all the people I know, the person I want to talk to most is John.

A person

He has found a place. A tiny boarded-up room in a disused house. The rest of the house is uninhabitable – full of twisted metal and open to the sky, but this small space has somehow stayed undiscovered. The entrance isn't visible from the roadside because a pile of rubble blocks the front door. He found a way in around the back where a sheet of corrugated iron had come loose. The room is dark, dank, concrete. The single window is glassless, but misty plastic sheeting has been nailed in. It is dry. It is a place where he can leave his things. He will find some cardboard to sleep on.

For the first time in years, he is inside! Not only that, but he is alone. Out of sight, he can shed a layer of hard skin and rest a little. Make his plans. For the moment to act is approaching and he must think and prepare.

He puts down his sack. It is a new one. He found it in a skip last week. Just a woven plastic feed sack, but still good. Useful. What makes it special is its English slogan, *A Gift from the American People*. He likes that. The bag might have come from George Bush himself. He takes his precious scraps of paper from the bag now.

While he was in the skip, fingering the small holes in the feedbag, he noticed something else. A magazine. An English-language magazine. He ripped a page from the magazine to keep. Now, in his small room, he unfolds it. He smooths it straight and looks about for a place to hang it. There is a nail by the window that is perfect. He thinks of the little children dancing on the carpet in the advertisement for the vacuum cleaner. If he had a carpet, he would dance now.

On the paper is written a list. If he closes his eyes, he can recite it by heart. It says:

1. A real man is strong
2. A real man is focused
3. A real man doesn't gossip
4. A real man's word is his bond
5. A real man makes his own fortune
6. A real man doesn't look like a woman
7. A real man keeps his house in order
8. A real man can defend himself
9. A real man knows the importance of family

He thinks of all the real men he knows of. There are not that many. Emperor Tewodros. There is a man called David Beckham he has heard people speak about. A white footballer. But he doesn't think football is as important as running a country, and besides, they say he looks like a woman. He prefers Wayne Rooney – short, squat, skilful. And George Bush. George Bush is a real man. He fails on number 5, but Mr Bush can't help it that his father was rich, any more than he himself can help having bees in his head. Nobody's perfect.

Someone put that magazine in the skip for him to find, the way they left the feed sack. It was a gift. A gift from George. George knew that he alone would be able to read it, would be able to grasp its import. It is a recognition of the fact that he is marked for great things.

The list makes him proud. He likes to run through it,

ticking off his qualities. There are other lists, he knows. The Ten Commandments, of course. But this is the list that speaks to him. It is George's list.

There have been men on the street who have not survived a single rainy season. Either they bit back their quarrels and went begging to relatives for a dry place to sleep, or they died, drowned drunk in a ditch, blanched by the *keremt* rains, damming the gutter with their swollen bodies. He is stronger than that. He doesn't get sick much. Only pains in his stomach. He can walk all day in bare feet with no food in his belly. *A man's stomach shall be satisfied from the fruit of his mouth, from the produce of his lips he shall be filled.*

Number 1, strength, is not a problem.

He is focused. Apart from the days when the radio static and bees crackle and buzz in his head, his only purpose is to walk, to observe and to prepare for what is coming. To make notes. It is a secret purpose (a real man doesn't gossip), but once read, it will offer guidance and insight to the most powerful. When he has got all his thoughts straight about the Ethiopian people, he will submit them to the prime minister. He does not hope to make a fortune. What would he do with money? Perhaps he will walk through the streets with it, handing it out to the poor. Will they recognise him when he is wearing a suit? Should he wear his face paint when he wears the suit?

A real man can defend himself. Once when he was sleeping the glue-sniffer boys came. He heard them coming shouting up the street, throwing stones at shacks, wild whooping. He pulled up his legs under his sheet of tin, but not fast enough. They saw him and came clustering. They wanted to play with him, they said. They rattled the tin sheet. *Come out! Come out!* Then they started throwing stones at the metal and each clang resounded through his head like he was inside a bell. They started throwing rocks. He felt one so big hit the tin that it dented and sagged. He would be buried alive. He unrolled from his foetal ball and lay on his back waiting for the next assault. When the rock struck, he leaped up, pushing the tin sheet towards the boys so that they stumbled back. He saw their eyes, wide and empty, apertures to the holes in their brains that the glue had eaten. He snarled at them like a dog and showed them his nails, madness his most effective defence. The younger of the boys, a teenager, turned and ran, but the others stood their ground. He growled at them, spilling spit from his mouth to show them what a crazy hound he could be. The boys stepped back. In a fury of rage, he launched himself at them, biting and scratching and tearing with his nails. The boys screamed and ran, but he hadn't even broken the skin when he bit. He could taste the soap from the warm brown skin of the eldest boy and he knew that despite the boy's addiction, he at least had a home to go to. There was something intimate in the taste of soap, the soft fuzz of hair. He spat the taste away.

Do his face-painting and his hair make him look womanly? He would be loathe to forego them, but he worries they do. But, he reassures himself, the Emperor Tewodros had long hair, and no one would have told *him* he looked womanly. Besides, the face paint is practice for the warpaint that all will wear when the time comes.

Last on the list is written – *A real man knows the importance of family*. He stares at that one. It fills him with unease. He would like to scratch it out. Perhaps he could just rip away that part of the paper. But a great blankness, an almost stupefying weight of sadness descends on him and he feels that the effort of raising his arm is too great.

He thinks of an old woman he knows, a woman in the market who has a different kind of madness from his. The woman lies stiff and still under huge rocks that she has carefully balanced along her body from shins to chest. The woman needs her rocks. Without them she is fretful, but when she lies beneath them, a small smile creases her black mouth. He knows the fear of floating untethered through life, but there is no comfort for him in such a crushing weight. He looks away from number 9, reminds himself to breathe, and heaviness falls from him. Memories of the rainy season, *keremt*. The sound of thunder in the hills; a distant crumbling rock fall. Number 9 is just a sentence on a list. The meaning of it will come to him.

He looks around the little room and begins to unpack. He stows his plastic bags in one corner. His refuge. His place. Mentally, he adds a sentence. A man needs a base. A base of operations.

He pushes aside the corrugated iron and slides out, making sure to block the entrance with a lump of concrete. Quietly he slips around the side of the room and around the pile of rubble. He perches there for a bit, watching the passers-by to see if they have observed him leaving. They are preoccupied with their own business. He smiles. George directed him to this place as a sign that the time to act is drawing near. Good. He is ready. Feeling lighter than he has done in years, his pen and pencil his only possessions, he sets off on his daily walk to the hospital.

Mariam

It is a quiet day on the ward today. Dr Tadesse and his herd of students have not yet arrived. Outside the door, fathers pace the corridors, loitering, lurching from sleep to accost doctors for news, but the doorman bars their entry to the ward. A few mothers hover in the critical care room, one breast out in perpetual milk expression, but here in the stable ward there is only a fat rhesus-incompatible baby under the blue bili lights. His mother sits with her eyes closed in a chair next to his crib. Outside it is a dry, breezy day, cool. Down below, the yellow pollen will be blowing from the cypress trees, making little drifts in the car park. The shoeshine boys will be touting for trade in the sunshine, while in the shade men sit with wheelbarrows of bananas, sugar cane and oranges.

I hold the baby close to my chest, feeling her translucent skin against my own. I don't really have a sense of her as a person. She is a bundle of cells, a ticking cog. A potential person. I don't really want to know her until I am sure she will survive.

The door opens. Nurse Rahel eases herself quietly into the room and pulls up a chair next to me. My friend is slim, with frail wrists and collarbones, a fine face with an Arab nose. I liked her the moment I first saw her, perhaps because we look so alike. We could almost pass for sisters, though I'm ten years older, a little fuller than her. Of course, the joke of our sisterhood faltered when I told her I was adopted. It was only when we'd ruled out the possibility of being related that we could really laugh.

She puts her finger to her lips and waits to take over her shift with the baby. I knew she would be up for this insane scheme. She is stubborn like me, resilient.

"*Salem nesh? Indet nesh? Baby, dehna nat?*" Are you well? How are you? How's the baby?

"*Awo. Baby dehna nat.*" The baby's fine.

"How do you find it?" she asks. "This kangaroo care?"

I laugh. I love the way she trills the 'r's' in 'kangaroo care'.

"It's really hard for me to just sit. It's probably very good for me though."

"It is *so* hard to just sit," Rahel agrees. "I want to be always doing something. I feel lazy, just sitting. I have to make lists of all the good we're doing. Stabilising her heart rate, making nerve connections," she recites, ticking them off on her fingers. "What else? Better thermal control, metabolic adaptation, better nutritional uptake. Did I forget anything?" She laughs. "She is a lucky child."

"She is, but then all these babies are lucky that they've got you working with them," I tell her. "And these mothers."

"Ha. Maybe I should tell them that. See what they say!"

"Rahel, you're so patient with them. Dealing with their anger, giving them little tasks, showing them that their bodies haven't failed. How do you do it?"

Rahel shrugs. She's not used to praise.

"They are scared. I do what I can to help them."

"But it's so hard. Day in, day out. How do you make sense of all this suffering? What does it all mean?"

"God knows. He does. I believe that. It's not that I have got used to the suffering. Only that I accept it. Yes, many die, but some live. So I focus on the living ones and I know, because of how tired I feel, that at least I am doing my best." She speaks softly. "The ones who die can rest in heaven, in the arms of the angels." She takes my hand. "I wish you would come with me to church. Give the saints the problem and let them take the weight of your questions. There is comfort in religion."

I smile apologetically.

"I loved the churches in Gondar. The angels on the ceiling. So beautiful. But so disapproving."

"Ah, well, you can always tell the sinners in an Ethiopian painting; they turn a half-face to the painter. Did you see? The Arab invaders show only their profiles. If only Jesus could have had the eye of an artist, he'd have known Judas!"

"What's the name of that cannibal in the paintings? All fat and white, eating a severed arm?"

"Belai, Belai the cannibal. When a beggar pleaded for a drop of water in the name of the Virgin Mary, he gave her just one drop and his soul was saved."

"Redemption. So there's hope for me yet," I joke.

"I think there is a place in heaven for you, Mariam," she smiles, stroking my arm.

"Are you still dating Yohannes?" I ask.

"*Awo*," she affirms, inhaling the word in the Ethiopian way, as if making thrifty use of breath. "But I am thinking of finishing it," she says, frowning and lowering her voice. "He is not serious. He only ever seems to want me for one thing. I went to the doctor. I got the implant, you know, in case of any mistakes. They say it lasts a couple of years. I don't want a baby yet. And definitely not with him. I told myself it was the modern thing to do. But really I was just tired of the arguments about him wearing a condom. Oh my God, he was so happy. But since I got the implant, I worry I will catch something from him. I don't want to find out he's unfaithful like that."

"Oh, Rahel, you can do so much better than Yohannes. Why don't you finish it?"

"I know," she sighs. "But, after a long shift, especially when a child has died on the ward, sometimes I just need to lie in someone's arms. I *should* end it. I will. When his next exam is over. I don't want to be blamed for making him fail."

The baby twitches. Little barometer. She is all empathy – every feeling made flesh affects her. How will she survive out there?

"Right, child. Time to move," I say.

I extract her from my shirt where she has been nestling. She stiffens, but does not protest. Quickly, Rahel undoes her top and we switch places. She takes my seat; I place the baby against her skin and she covers its back with a blanket.

"In only a few weeks we will have to send this little one to the orphanage," says my friend, settling herself into the chair.

"Yes."

I look down at the top of the baby's head and watch a blue vein throbbing near her fontanelle. The down of hair that covered her body is receding and instead soft fur is growing on her scalp. The child pants a little and then is still. Her eyes are mostly closed now; she seems only to want to sleep when she is next to a body. Only then can she let her guard down. She is so small. The size of a kitten. If she were a kitten, she would have been drowned. A female too. A liability. Females keep getting pregnant and who wants to deal with the consequences of that? Perhaps someone will adopt her. Without the care we are giving her she'd be dead before the papers could be signed. Rahel sees my expression, takes my hand and smiles.

"Mariam. Most blessed lady." She strokes my hand, pulling the fingers gently one by one, then squeezing it tight. "You know, when you first arrived the doctors were sure you had a pot of money, a secret fund."

"Ha! Really?"

"Well, you never know with these foreigners. After all, many years ago, Dr John brought in funds and equipment. I heard they wanted to name a ward after him, but he refused."

"Well, sorry to disappoint," I laugh. "I did try to fix the toilets."

"Oh, Mariam, you didn't disappoint. You reminded us of the things we already had. Skin, warmth, love. Mothers."

"You're kind to me."

"Ah, yes, *I* am. But, you know, the paediatricians don't like you! You get them to make promises and then force them to keep them. You ignore their stupid battles with each other. Also, you are always making them sign your little bits of paper."

I chuckle wryly.

"Don't despair, *Mariame*. We are buying her a little time. Perhaps she will be strong enough," says my friend.

I reach out and place my hand over the baby's fragile skull. The baby shifts her weight, startling.

Rahel shushes.

"Shh, shh, little one. Don't complain. Among all of us, you have been blessed."

Dr Tadesse

His wife is shouting at him on the phone. Really shouting. He has to hold the handpiece away from his ear. She should have some self-control. She'll be hitting him next.

"Shh," he tells her, "shh." He will have to step outside the ward if she keeps this up. He was out late last night at the Alize bar and his head aches. But jazz is his passion. How he wept when the jazz club at the old Hotel Taitu burned down. So much history. Such a waste. She knew about his passions when she married him. He is a passionate man. Did she think he would be home every night writing research papers and massaging her feet? Perhaps they should have dated for longer. Got to know each other better. She was keen to have a big wedding, the white dress and the limousine, and he let himself be rushed along, thinking of her red lips and the curve of her fine firm behind. She thinks he is unfaithful to her, probably. She's wrong. Music is his only mistress. He loses himself in the swoony melodic scales, in the close brass and the off-kilter rhythms of the piano. It's only once a week. A man needs an outlet. She has her life, he his. Or is he not allowed to live anymore?

"*Beka*!" he snaps. Enough! He hangs up.

The doorman scowls at him and motions silence.

"What?" he mimes. Can he not speak his mind on his own ward?

He should not have had that second cup of coffee. It

sluiced right through him; he needs to shit but he'll have to hold it in now until the ward round is finished. He feels shaky. What kind of Ethiopian can't drink coffee? He doesn't feel responsible enough to be doing this job today; sometimes the enormity of what he does for a living (if you can call it that) overwhelms him and he'd like to hide in bed with his head under the covers. They ask too much of him. He puts on a brave face of course, and he knows his stuff. But what's the point in knowing your stuff, if what you know is that this baby needs an urgent heart operation, but there is no one in the country qualified to do the surgery? Perhaps it would be better to be ignorant like the mothers with their holy water and their anxious round eyes. He can't bear it when they look at him as if he's personally let them down. He'd rather they rail at God than blame the messenger.

He sits in the corridor with a pile of notes. The students have begun to drift in, after their morning meeting. He's glad to see a few women students among them. You get a different viewpoint from a female doctor. Subtler. They think about the little things, like bothering to ask the mother how the baby is. They notice things that even he fails to see. Of course, by the end they are harder, more masculine than the male doctors. Cattier too. They bear grudges. He's still trying to work out where he went wrong with the head of Obs and Gyne. She intimidates the hell out of him with her grey helmet of hair and her imposing bosom. She won't answer his calls and her secretary fobs him off with some excuse or other.

He looks over the notes for today's critical babies. A few interesting cases. One born with his gut outside his body. Another born with no anus; probably Down's as well. That's a nasty operation. A few hypothermics. Twins. In the stable room, there's a jaundiced baby, one with neurological problems and then there's Mariam's baby. She and that pretty nurse Rahel have finished their ridiculous kangaroo care shifts for the day and the child is back in the incubator where she belongs. Why Mariam is putting so much time into that baby he does not know. They're soft, these *ferenj*. Not realistic. Of course he would like to help every baby, but there are too many of them.

He knows she ridicules him. The more he tries to earn her respect, the more she smiles that faintly supercilious smile. 'What are you trying to prove, Dr Tadesse?' it says. She thinks he's lazy, callous. What she doesn't realise is that you have to find your activity level. He's known doctors at the hospital burn out after a few years. They get cynical, exhausted. Mostly they go into private practice, tending to the rich diaspora's kids for constipation and eczema. A lucky few get work overseas. He could join them if he wanted; he's had offers. But he's turned them down. That's what he'd like Mariam to know. He's chosen to stay to help his country. So let her raise her eyebrows at his sponsored conference lunches. He goes to court the suppliers and get cheaper drugs for the patients, not to enjoy the rare beef and pavlova, whatever she thinks. Who did she think she was, paying to fix the toilets on the labour ward? That is not the way things work here and he will tell her so.

There is something phoney about a midwife doing skin-to-skin. Not from the child's point of view, of course, he can see that the child benefits, but from the midwife's. It's a proxy love. A going-through-the-motions love. There is something distasteful about it to him. How can you hold a baby next to your skin without it touching your heart? What sort of person is so hard, so protected, that she can hand that child back without dying inside every time? He hopes for her sake that she will get hurt, taking on that baby. Because it should hurt. And that's why he keeps his distance, why all the sane doctors do. That desire to not be hurting all the time. Part of him wants to override her and send the thing to the orphanage to die its inevitable death. Sooner or later it will have to happen. He doesn't like it under his nose. There should be equality of care. Why this child?

The students have gathered and he rouses himself to action, keeping a tight grip on his sphincter and the coffee grounds that swirl within. They line up to wash their hands then troop into the critical room. He eyes them critically.

With the first years, it's all theory. They are going to change the world, transform their country, or even better buy themselves a ticket to the States to practice in Atlanta or Miami. The second and third years are more serious; they've started doing ward rounds and have seen the scale of the problem. Although they respect their elders and betters, the professors like himself who guide the little flitting shoals of observers round the wards, they still have hope that they'll do better, that their new world of smart phones and Facebook will somehow imbue them with the edge to once and for all stop the ancient diseases that ravage their people.

The interns and the residents are exhausted. Proud that they have gone the distance, but you see the seeds of fear. They cloak themselves in the unapproachable arrogance of doctors everywhere who hold the lives of their patients in their hands. They must decide to operate, or to let a patient slip away, in the knowledge that elsewhere in the world a piece of equipment that costs less than a few cups of coffee could have saved them.

The mothers flinch and huddle as the ward round

approaches; they'd like to ask questions but they form a unit of suffering instead; they have no rights here. They must take it on trust that their babies are being cared for. They must think themselves lucky that such educated people are here to examine their children. In the countryside, their babies would be dead.

The child with the gut born outside his body has a fever; it means that an infection has already set in. His gut, pink and flaccid, has been wrapped in clingfilm. If they had been able to operate soon after he was born, he might have stood a good chance, but for every hour the operation is delayed the odds of survival diminish. And now he has an infection they cannot operate. He handles the child brusquely, wearing imaginary gloves that will protect him from the presence of death. The students cluster respectfully round while the mother, one breast out, methodically milks herself in a gesture than reminds him of flagellates. The child with no anus is beautiful; he has the slanting eyes of a Down's child. The condition is obvious to anyone, but as usual they have left it to him to inform the mother. He'll do it later and watch her downcast eyes as she wonders what she did for God to punish her and her child. The child has a single crease across each palm, another mark. If he lives, he will be simple. A life trapped in a dark hut. But he will probably not survive. Perhaps it is for the best.

The twins are coping well. Their mother is cup-feeding one her milk while the doctors examine its sister. The babies without mothers are mute bundles, waiting for a sign to stay or depart their little lives.

They move to the stable room and he feels a sense of rising unease; he does not want to touch Mariam's baby. He examines the jaundiced baby. Its bilirubin levels have gone down and it will be discharged later today. The mother is delighted; she holds his sleeve and thanks him, praising God. Doctor, God. One must be careful not to let it go to one's head. God punishes those doctors with hubris, he reminds them of their fallibility. His own brother was killed in a car accident two years ago. The doctors could not save him. He moves on. The baby with neurological problems is stable. Perhaps its problems are the result of the forceps that left broad bruises at its temples. Perhaps the problems will resolve with time.

Mariam's baby is lying on her back. He lifts the lid of the incubator and she shivers. She has put on a little weight. Her skin is still translucent, but there are fat deposits that make her face less pinched. She is a pretty child. Rosebud mouth and neat features. He cannot bring himself to touch her. It feels indecent, like it is Mariam's flesh he is touching.

"Tigist, why don't you examine this child?" he suggests to a surprised intern. He picks a woman because this is a child brought into a world of women. Born to one, warmed by two others, fed with the milk of yet another. Tigist handles her gently, but for all her prematurity, the child protests. She stiffens and arches, wincing and mewling like a kitten. Ingrate, thinks Tadesse. Why does he find this child so distasteful? It is a project child, he reasons. Not for itself is it kept alive, but to prove a point. A lesson to the hospital in what it lacks; time and love. Well, fuck you, Mariam. You can only do so much. Your proxy love only goes so far. We love all our children; we weep blood for them. Don't come here to teach us love before you've known the pain of loss. It's only because you're hard that you have the capacity to hold that child.

The child is healthy. She is ready to come off the tube and

be cup fed. He delivers a little speech to the students about the superior powers of breastmilk, about the miraculous powers of skin-to-skin. The students nod. The overwhelming urge to defecate overtakes him and he calls the ward round to a close, taking the stairs to the paediatricians' floor two at a time.

Mariam

On the way to Betty's I get stuck in a jam. The kind of jam the new Chinese tram system was meant to do away with. Menelik had his Europeans, Selassie his Japanese. Now the government is courting China. Funny, the Chinese in Ethiopia. They roam in packs. You only ever see them in gaggles, heading construction teams, in the expat supermarkets, or on the one occasion I went to a club near Chechnya, perching on the padded banquets being stroked and cajoled by prostitutes. I don't know what they think of Africans, or whether they give a monkey's about the development of the continent, but they get things done. Seble mutters that what they build won't last, but I think the fact that they build it shows it's possible. Perhaps that's a good incentive to progress. Ethiopia has always been a nation of mountain hermits with riches, but no roads to transport them. That's what the Chinese are giving them.

For the people, though, it's not China they adore. It's America. That's where the wealthy and the intelligentsia fled to when the Derg took power. And now some of them and their children are returning to the motherland, beef-fed, with good teeth and conspicuous wealth. Haile Selassie would be so proud. The Americans label their aid sacks proudly, *A Gift from the American People*, whereas we British, with our traditional reserve, quietly fund Ethiopian organisations. You'd think America was single-handedly funding relief in this country sometimes.

We're in gridlock. I sigh and slump back. The Ethiopians are better at waiting than me. They've had whole lives of practice. The cars inch forward, lurching over potholes. Faces stare blankly from the blue Hiace minibuses. Blue donkeys, they call them. The drivers hire them by the hour so they take the most lethal risks to get fares. They nose their way into unfeasible spaces and drive far too fast and too close together. It's mostly them, with their selfish driving, causing the jams. Belarusian trucks full of rocks spout black fumes that mean my window has to stay tight shut despite the afternoon heat. My taxi driver isn't the talkative type. His tiny battered Toyota must be forty years old. It's held together with bits of string and tape, but although a bit dusty, it's clean. He's put a strip of pink fake fur and some plastic roses on the back window ledge. From the rear-view mirror hang two cardboard decorations: the Virgin Mary and the Arsenal cannon.

The Emirates Stadium is just down the road from the Whittington hospital. It's hard to imagine going back to the ward where I worked before, let alone being in charge. They told me I was crazy to do VSO at this stage in my career. That'd I fall off the radar. But I wanted to do it and it looks like it's paid off. Coming to Ethiopia means that I can look my colleagues in the eye. I am torn between thinking how ecstatic I will be back at the Whitt to have stocks of syringes and plasters and sanitary towels to dole out, and worrying that I will want to slap the mothers for being ungrateful for the clean hospital, the free care. Obviously, I would never actually slap them, though I've occasionally seen doctors do it here. They've told me afterwards that it's a tactic to get active labour going, that it shocks the mother into pushing, but

I'm not sure I believe them. I think some of them regard the mothers as over-fertile time-wasters, blocking up good beds.

I used to bike to work past the Emirates Stadium, slogging up Holloway Road on frosty mornings, past the grim estates that spread towards Hornsey, charting the gradual increase in affluence as the old road rises up out of the fumes and into breezy, moneyed Highgate. Of course, I never got as far as Highgate; the Whittington sits between the stained concrete and kebab shops of Archway and the delis and bistros of the Village. But a few of the Highgate mums used the hospital, so when I was doing postnatal check-ups I'd get the odd cup of Darjeeling to offset all the Typhoo. To be honest, I didn't much care if I was in a bedsit on the Andover estate or in a drawing room near Waterlow Park; a baby's a baby. Given the schedules, I hardly had time to take in my surroundings anyway.

The best bit about riding my bike was the long swoosh down the hill at the end of the day. It used to return me to myself; clear out the fumes of surgical spirit and the rich reek of blood. It would be suicide to ride a bike here in Addis; the cars and trucks and minibuses are so tightly packed you'd never get through. And it's not like there are many ambulances to pick you up if you got knocked off either.

There's a scrabbling at my window. An old lady with no teeth is raising her hands to me. Can she see me, or is she blind? I decide she's adopted the not-seeing thing that I do with the babies. Don't get over-involved or it'll hurt. Whether a hand passes coins out to you or not, you don't want a relationship with that person. I reach in my bag and hand her all I can find, about 45 cents. She blesses me with a toothless smile before resetting her face into its mask of pitifulness and moving on.

When I get back to London, what will the other midwives ask me about Ethiopia? Will they ask me anything at all? Perhaps they'll resent me for having got away. Or think I've had an extended gap year. Women can be worse than men when it comes to petty envy, to passive aggression. Projecting their discontent onto others. Many of the best ones were already thinking of leaving midwifery. Worn down by the paperwork, the responsibility, the lack of time with each patient. It's not why they went into the job. Some will have become private midwives, tending to the Highgate ladies with their IVF twins and their maternity nurses to do the night feeds. Others will have taken early retirement. That leaves the hardened ones, the workhorses, the least sensitive ones for me to manage. I sigh loudly, making my taxi driver start. The car inches forward.

I stare out the window at the shuddering side of a stationary truck. Have I really achieved anything here? What mark did I leave? The phrase makes me think of the relief marks of those Hiroshima victims, the shapes of their bodies left on the pavements when the bomb dropped. A Mariam-shaped mark. What would that look like? I think of T'irunesh, and the episiotomy they wanted to do, the needless cut I prevented them from making to get the baby out. Leaving something unmarked... that can be a kind of mark, I suppose.

The taxi sees a space and revs into it, catapulting me backwards. Suddenly we've escaped the chaos and are rattling along the highway to Betty's. I resolve not to think about the Whittington again. I'll be back there soon enough. The time will evaporate and Ethiopia will be hard to imagine. I get a pain in my chest and I rub my hand across my heart where I assume the seat belt is, before I realise that of course there are no seat belts in an Addis taxi.

It's Wednesday, fasting day, and Betty's cooking up *beyenetu*, a huge pot of spinach *wot*, *shiro*, potato and carrot stew, split pea stew and spongy rolls of *injera*. The kids are watching satellite TV and the baby's playing with the nanny. We can talk.

She folds her arms and leans back when I tell her about John. She's pensive. I was hoping she'd diss him and call him names, and I could cover my shame. Instead, she looks sad for me and I feel humiliated. She fingers a long strand of dread-locked hair, and twiddles the silver clip that grips the end.

"He's a good man," she says eventually.

"For not breaking my heart? I realise I hardly know him, but it is a bit broken."

"Not nearly as much as it would have been. And to know himself so well. That's unusual. I mean, how many men are going to pass up the chance of a night with beautiful Mariam?"

"Maybe he's impotent," I suggest sulkily.

"Mariam, stop it. He liked you, and you're leaving. I like this man. If I knew him, I'd ask him round for dinner."

"Well, don't invite me. I don't want to see him."

"Don't you?"

"Of course I do." I sigh, dropping the pretence. "I keep thinking of things I want to tell him. Things I wished I asked him. But I don't want to see him if I have to pretend that everything is hunky-dory. I like him a lot. It's been a while since I liked someone. I let myself imagine..."

"What?" says Betty, piercing me with her dark eyes.

"Some kind of relationship."

Betty narrows her eyes.

"Would he make a good father?"

"Betty! We only had one date! It's a bit early to be thinking about that!" I laugh.

But Betty isn't laughing.

"Why? How do you think anyone has children? After years of planning and conversations and ticking all the boxes? No, Mariam, children get made, if you want them in your life they come to you. You're thirty-six. Do you not want children?"

"I don't know. Maybe. Someday. I mean, I like babies. I work with them enough."

I want to remind her that any baby I might have would be the first blood relation I have ever known. This is too big a conversation to be having. I feel a bit persecuted. I hardly know the man. Should I really be thinking about our blond, brown-skinned, freckly children?

"Working with them isn't the same. Close your eyes, Mariam."

I snort, but she's serious. I close my eyes, making a 'this is ridiculous' face.

"Feel in your belly. Is there a space? Is there a place where a child could be? Do you feel the need for a child of your own, Mariam?"

Bloody Betty and her hippy nonsense. I feel patronised. She has no right to push me on this, but I breathe and tell myself that she means well. Against my better judgement, I try to feel something. I think about the abandoned baby in the incubator, and how her body moves against my chest. I try to imagine if she was mine. I imagine taking her out of the hospital and bringing her home and promising her that I will never leave her. But the feeling I get is not in my belly but in my chest; a shortness of breath and a panic. How can you love like that? How can you promise to love someone for ever? How can you give yourself like that, in trust? My mother, my birth mother could not love me like that. She gave me away to the orphanage when I was a year old. Not on the first day, in panic, but after a year. She knew me, and still she gave me up. If she had loved me, surely she would have kept me, begged with me on her back at the side of the road. I see those women with their toddlers. The women are haggard, but the toddlers look healthy and happy, tugging on their mother's breast, playing with a plastic bottle in the dust. She would not have given me up if she loved me. So perhaps it was for the best that she gave me away, just as it is for the best that I never bear children. Leave the love and the vulnerability for those who have a talent for it.

"Do you feel it in your belly, Mariam?" says Betty.

"No," I say simply. I stand up and get my coat. We haven't eaten yet but suddenly I feel like I can't be in this house any longer. "Is it such a big deal if I don't want a child?" I say to Betty through the lump in my throat.

"Hey," she says, "I was just trying to open this up. Stay, *Mariame*. I'm sorry, I shouldn't have pressured you. I just want you to be happy."

"I am happy," I tell her, "happy enough. Why do people need a child to complete their life? I think it says a lot about how inadequate their lives are. I think you should think about your own life. What hole are you filling with your kids? Is it the fact that Solomon's never here?"

"That's hard," she says, shocked at my bitchiness. "That's a hard thing to say, Mariam."

"Is it? Well, maybe I get more done by being hard. I can make my own choices, Betty."

I step into the street feeling bereft. Not only have I fought with my best friend, who loves me, but now I am hungry, pitiful, single and childless to boot. I hail a rattling cab and we edge out into the traffic as the late sun glowers through the fumes.

A person called Tewodros

PENTAGON, WASHINGTON, DC washing machine. Liverpool Everton ISRAEL A former member of the Soviet Union Omo powder For you have delivered my soul from death, keep my soul and deliver me. UNHCR. Ethiopian Red Cross. Care. Cure. Save the Children. UNICEF. Mercy Corps. Christian Aid. Solomon, Mark, Abraham, Ezekiel, Isiah, Chevrolet, Suarez, Paul, Bertukan Mubrak Misrak Mohammed Tsehay Ali Daniel Getachew Fisum Tabor Eskidat Kifle Amon, Josiah, Jecomiah, Shealtiel, Zerubabel, Abiud, Eliakim, Acorzadok. Galaxy Night Star Balcha Hospital 01 54 84 58 3020 Volvo Armenia Sporting school Arrafat FAITH IS LIFE. LIVE IN FAITH. DRIVE IN FAITH. I belong to Jesus. Television, World vision Cure Hospital for children Elizabeth Arden Desert storm wind storm H20 31511 St George's dermatology clinic Sandford International school Drink water from your own cistern and running water from your own well. USAID Net weight 50 kg PS54 24-22. Not for repackaging. Not for sale or exchange.

He collects his words on his scraps of paper like the woody eucalyptus seeds he collected as a child. The seeds, hard blue-green discs, filled his drawers until the room smelled like a sick house. His brother made him throw them away. But these words take up less room than the seeds had done. They are both exciting and reassuring. Writing them down helps to quiet the babble in his head. They speak of the wider world, the connection between people. Seeing the words on the page gives him certainty about his life. About his mission. Everything is connected. George the Father. George the Son. George the Holy Ghost.

He is so busy reading that he almost stumbles over the dead dog lying at the side of the road. It must have been hit by a car. Its mouth is leering open in a terrible grin. Its belly is swollen as if it is pregnant, but he can see it is a male dog when the buzzing swarm rises from its engorged genitals. Its legs stick out straight as if it is stretching.

He will have to pass it, but it scares him. In the twilight, he has watched a pile of sleeping dogs uncurl themselves, then uncurl and uncurl until out of the pile that he had thought only four dogs, ten or fifteen had emerged, grinning and scratching and sniffing, claiming their city. What if this dog were to suddenly burst into life, and come running at him with those wide-open jaws? A long time ago his mother told him about rabies, the mad sickness. If you are bitten, your mouth starts making froth, and water scares you. How could someone be scared of water? The idea is so ridiculous it sends him blank with fear. The fear takes him back to another dead dog, a dog from years before. How many generations of dog have interceded between this one and the one he faced as a schoolboy? It is as if yesterday and he is suddenly back there.

A crowd of school children is coming up behind him. He must pass the dead dog or face ridicule. In his short trousers, he can even see the shake in his knees. He puts one foot in front of the other, but with each step the woozy feeling overtakes him and he knows a fit is coming. It is as seductive as it is sickening. He is falling into its embrace. A gap of time in which the angels speak to him and he will wake bruised and ashamed with wet pants. The sky is beneath his feet, shining and full of stars and he is standing on his head on a precipice of tarmac. How many minutes have passed since the fit took him? He hears through his right ear the approach of the children and the worried mutter of adults. Someone is lifting him upside down by his feet; it makes the blood rush to his head so that he feels his skull will burst like the dead dog's guts. The throbbing subsides and he is lying on the road. When he wakes, the first thing he sees is the dog's astonished eye observing him. He scrambles back.

"Urgh! He's peed in his pants!" yells a boy. "Run! He'll get you!" They dash off, laughing. An adult hand helps him to his feet.

"*Aizoh.* There, there. How are you feeling? You've had an attack before?" He nods at the older gentleman, who looks shaken. "Do you need to go home to your mother? Change your trousers?"

He shakes his head and gestures to the bag that contains a spare pair of trousers and pants.

"You should take a rest. Sit down. Tell your teacher."

He nods and walks slowly towards the school with his head low.

Why does he get these attacks? They started a few years before. The first one was the day his father came home on army leave. Everyone said it was because he got overexcited.

But then he had one the next week too. He's known for a while that if he rubs his nose in a certain way so that the shadow of his fingers flickers past his closed lids he can lose his sense of time and place. He does it in bed at night. Across the room, under the sheets, his elder brother prefers fumbling with his dick, but he rubs his nose. It is not that he wants to escape his life; he likes his family. He loves his mother and his grandparents. But the feeling he gets when the fits come on is like standing on a tall peak, whipped by a cool wind. *Open my eyes, oh Lord, that I may see marvellous things*. He is swept up to the peak on eagle's wings and the ascent draws the breath from his lungs and leaves cool ether in its place. He can see the shape of things, the world spread below him. He is not inculcated in the squalor and scrabble and laughter, but clean, alone and serious. When someone gives him a book about the Emperor Tewodros, his namesake, he knows he shares something of that great king's prescience.

His mother takes him to doctors who keep him in hospital overnight to observe him. Nothing happens, except that he stays awake staring at the grey face of a boy who's had his leg amputated. A sight that gives him nightmares for weeks afterwards. They send him home with him some pills to take, but they make him feel sleepy and sick and prevent him from going to school. He stops taking them. For a while his mother walks with him into school, but the other boys laugh so he tells her to stay home. She draws him to her warm body and pulls his head to her breasts. She smells of soap and sweat and frankincense. She tells him that God will protect him and she packs him spare trousers. She has her aunt's berbere stall to take care of.

He is a model pupil. They call him the little doctor for his interest in science. Maybe, they say, he will become a doctor and invent a cure for his ailment. He smiles, but what they cannot understand is that he feels blessed by his condition. It sets him apart; to lose the sweet moments of soaring bliss and descend to the mundanity of life would drain the colour from his life. He feels himself excelling at science and it scares him. He must protect his hilltop from the cure he will be compelled to find, so he switches his attention to language.

The children all learn English. They have primers with pictures of fruit and animals and long sentences to copy out. They repeat by rote the teacher's lines on the blackboard. The hardest words to say are *this* and *there* and *they*. His tongue wants to feel the sharp vibration of a 'z': 'ziz', 'zere', 'zey'. The teacher makes them stick out their tongues in a way that is almost obscene, to emphasise the fat floppiness of the sound. It feels uncouth. Pink tips of tongues protruding. He likes to form the present perfect. 'I have been', 'I have gone'; he likes the way the tense collects experience, completes it and packs it away. In his own life, he yearns for such completion. The room he shares with his brother is small and he never has enough room to store all the things he wants to collect.

When his father comes home from service in the north, the house is temporarily more ordered. He is paraded as the bright boy and his brother kicks him under the table. His learning compensates for the fits. The soldier father rubs his son's head. Tewodros's hair is close cropped and his forehead high and broad. He pulls the boy's ear lobes. His father has jug ears and the broad smiling mouth of a farmer, which his father and his father's father had been. Even though he is a soldier, he still spits in his hand in the traditional way before he shakes with his neighbours. Unlike his ancestors, he has seen the country.

He has travelled up to the hot highlands where the mountaintops have been cut off by God, forming plateaus that overlook the whole of Ethiopia. On the tops of those mountains are tiny hidden churches, his father tells him. The priests are so ancient that perhaps, years ago, in their youth, they built the churches themselves, with the angels' help, of course. Some of the churches are hidden inside caves, and the fleas that riddle them are sent direct from the devil to distract you from your prayers! Once he climbed up Debre Damo on a long rope and saw paintings that made him weep. The thought of climbing down that rope again, with its terrifying view of the hard rock below, almost made him weep too. He looks deep into his son's eyes and shakes his head. Later, the boy overhears him saying to his wife that though he trusts her more than the *abuna* himself he sees none of himself in there. He confides that he had an uncle who was touched. The uncle became a priest.

"Perhaps the boy... ?" suggests his mother.

"No," declares his father. "He does too well at school to pull him out to learn nothing but the old stories."

His face clouds. They will have to trust that in the new world that is coming there will be a softness, an indulgence, a place for such as his son.

At school, the dog and the fit forgotten, the boy enjoys writing his name, again and again. Tewodros. Tewodros. The 'w' absorbed into the word like the little leap of nothing lost to fits. Despite the swallowed centre the word is whole and satisfying. Was he named for the emperor? He doesn't think to ask. He is often Teddy at home.

He likes to write. There is something about the lines on the page that gives him immense satisfaction. Sometimes the teachers have to turn him out of class to play; the lines lead him on. If he followed them to their conclusion, he feels he would learn something of great use.

Children have short memories. With clean trousers, he is accepted into their games of football and climbing. Sometimes he goes for weeks between fits, and then he is like the others: scabby knees, a pocket full of stones, in his mind the secret place where they'd hidden the dead bird to see the skeleton it would make. Not quite like the others though; the others like to catch the girls and squeeze their arms to make them squeal. Some like to press their lips hard onto the girl's before thrusting her away and running. The girls are serious; they've been taught young to protect their dignity from such attacks. Their dignity is their life. Sometimes they cry. He doesn't want that. The thought of the sudden rush of scent from skin and hair, the softness of skin, makes him feel woozy as if the sickness were coming over him. He stays at the edge of the playground and writes in his book when they play those games.

Too soon his father is preparing to leave again, returning to the north where there have been skirmishes at the border with Eritrea. The army has begun to mass troops near the town of Badme. His regiment is posted near Mekele, but might be moved any day. A big meal is cooked to mark his leaving. Aunts arrive, in floating cheesecloth dresses, their hair intricately plaited. Uncles come bringing bottles of honey *tej* and home-made *tella* beer. His mother squats out the back, preparing dish after dish. Some of the aunts squeeze his father's hand and exhort him in the name of God to stay safe. His father laughs, his broad face creasing, his wide, gapped teeth shining under the bare bulb of their front room.

The priest arrives. He has a sour face beneath the great pile of white turban he wears. His beard is wispy over features as wizened as an old root. He draws out his silver cross and everyone takes turns to bow and kiss it. When it is Tewodros's turn, he sees his father look significantly to the priest. As he bows to kiss the cross, feeling it warm from the lips of his relatives, the priest takes him by the shoulder. He puts his hand under the boy's chin and looks deep into his eyes. Tewodros feels alarmed, but his father signals that he should submit.

"Your father tells me you have the devil in you, boy. That the devil overwhelms you from time to time. We must prevent him coming with prayer. You must resist. It is your duty to resist and trust in the good Lord Jesus Christ, do you hear? Only he can save you from sin. It is your weakness that allows the devil in. You must take holy water for your cure. If the madness comes, your mother is to bring you to me and we will scare away your demon with the power of our Lord."

Then he begins to intone some words in Ge'ez, guttural, ancient. Tewodros's father looks away, too embarrassed to meet his son's eye, but when the chanting is finished and the women bustle Tewodros away he sees his father slip the priest a handful of notes. His father looks flushed and relieved.

One of the uncles plays the *masinko* and another has a drum. The women begin to clap and his father begins to dance, a slow shuffling dance at first, as if shrugging his shoulders at the strangeness of life. The music gathers momentum and the women ululate, his father throws back his head and lifts and drops his shoulders in the rhythmic *eskista* style. An aunt steps up to dance with him, her huge breasts leaping and falling as they bounce her chains of silver and amber beads up to her chin. They look into each other's eyes, smiling, challenging as they circle each other, bare feet making patterns on the earth floor.

Tewodros keeps back. He does not want to dance. His body is not predictable like theirs; not just the fits, but the adolescent height he is trying to get used to, the way his body seems to have elongated. He cannot keep up with it. It is fortunate that he does not speak much, because even his voice betrays him with a squeak of late.

He is wedged into a corner with the heaving bodies of his family in front of him. As they clap and move he feels the throb in his blood responding. One of the aunts has been preparing the coffee ceremony and the reek of frankincense makes him feel his head will explode. A tall uncle is standing in front of the light bulb and with every movement he blocks the light, then reveals it; the light becomes the drumming and he has to close his eyes. Still behind his eyelids he sees the flicker and he knows a fit is unavoidable. He squats in the corner to buffer the fall and feels the black pressure building, the thrill of asphyxia and release.

When he wakes, all the guests are gone. The room is dark but for a candle. His father is watching him. Someone has placed blankets under and over his body; he feels beneath them to discover he is trouserless. Another humiliation. Across the room his father is watching him. He cannot read his father's expression, but he fears it is angry. He tries to find his voice, to apologise, but his tongue is fat and he feels like he has swallowed dust. Without warning his father stands and blows out the candle and retreats into the dark. His last image of his father is one of an angry icon; a face of polished wood, lips pouting before the flame.

He blinks. The children are coming out of school now and Tewodros, a grown man now, smiles to see their little legs in their little shorts and their big backpacks. He has been rooted to the spot, the spot near the dead dog, for a long while. A group come jostling down the pavement and he moves to show them his notebook. He has been writing his lessons too. Education never stops. We must always question and reflect. Listen to the words of our elders. He supposes that he must be considered an elder now. It has been years since he left school. The children scatter into the road, pulling each other by the hand. He catches the appalled scared face of one of the younger ones and he remembers what kind of man he has become. He stands for a while staring at his calloused feet. His one sandal. When he crumples the paper into a ball, his black nails are too long to make fists.

John

The morning meetings are meant to be to discuss client cases; a way to share knowledge and do handovers on the patients we share. They're casual affairs; no more than four or five of us usually. We senior doctors don't bother discussing the run-of-the-mill cases. It would be insulting to go over the textbook cases. It tends to be the babies with multiple conditions, birth abnormalities or unusual syndromes whose patient notes we bring to the table. We're usually in and out in half an hour. But as soon as I walk in to the meeting room I realise that today is going to be different and I wonder whose head will be on the block.

It's a large strip-lit seminar room with a central table, its varnished veneer chipped and split. It's broad enough that a fist aimed across it would fall short, not that Ethiopians are prone to physical outbursts. There are more subtle, painful ways to wound. The senior Obs and Gyne staff is all there; old Mulugeta with his puffy face and pursed lips won't meet my eye, but it could be that he's just worked the night shift. Idris, a tall, spindly Afar, one of the administrators I've known for years, gives me a significant look, the significance of which is lost on me. Is it a warning, or is there gloating there too? The paediatric team are huddled in one corner and I spot Tadesse in deep Amharic conversation with one of the surgeons, a small, skinny man named Getachew. Getachew's a good surgeon and keeps himself out of hospital politics.

Tadesse's height makes him stoop and he has pinned him in place with one large bony hand that seems to weigh on his shoulder as if he would plant him in the ground. He sees me at the door and breaks into an unconvincing smile. A relieved Getachew is released. I see him rubbing his bruised shoulder when he thinks no one is looking. Tadesse gestures me to sit next to him, but I sit opposite instead. I want to be able to read the expression on his face.

We start discussing cases. Not much to report; the Pierre-Robin Sequence child born a few days ago is still alive, though not feeding well. A baby with NEC died in the night from abdominal bleeding. Life and death. Statistics. Learning points. It's a funny old game. On we go. More babies. Some alive, some dead. The files of notes are worked through systematically until the last one. Tadesse coughs loudly and raises a hand.

"There are a number of issues I need to raise concerning our VSO midwife."

Around the table there is a moment of expectant hush and stillness from my colleagues that breaks suddenly into an almost comic wave of displacement activity; nose blowing, pencils dropped, casual stretching. Has he spoken to each one in turn, then? I smile, but I am tensing myself for a blow.

"A most unprofessional episode has been brought to my attention, regarding the use of private funds to repair hospital facilities. We must assume her ignorance in hospital procedure in this case, but I want to assure you all that I shall be discussing the issue with Sister Mariam."

A few nods. Mariam's toilets have clearly put a few noses out of joint.

"I've already mentioned it to her, Dr Tadesse," I say.

That took the wind out of his sails. He was looking

forward to ticking her off.

"I see. And her response?"

"She understands that it was inappropriate."

He looks piqued. Looks down at his notes. But he hasn't finished with Mariam yet.

"And then, of course, there is the issue of the premature baby, the abandoned baby currently under Dr John's supervision... Baby X, Merkato," he reads, as if the name were unfamiliar.

I raise my eyebrows at him. This is a betrayal of Mariam and he knows it.

"It seems that Sister Mariam has engaged in a lengthy project with this baby involving techniques of skin-to-skin warming and human milk."

I nod, and tilt my head. It was me who gave her permission to do her kangaroo care, to use her friend's breastmilk. Will it be my head on the block then?

I must concentrate if I am to protect her and her charge from this assault, but the repetition of her name, Mariam, keeps provoking a physical recall of our almost-closeness. To speak of her in this purely professional capacity feels like a betrayal of something too. It wasn't quite intimacy that we shared, but it was honesty perhaps. I drew a line when I turned her down. It was the right thing to do. The sensible thing. I shouldn't have asked her out in the first place. I should put her out of my mind. But she is here in the hospital and my mind keeps turning to her. The possibility of her. She might be my last chance. Three months isn't long, but could it be long enough to kindle something? Stop. Focus. I smile again.

'So what's you point, Tadesse?' my smile asks silently.

He gurns, uncomfortable.

"This is setting a precedent on the ward. This precedent

could be confusing to the nurses, and it may be damaging for the nurses involved, particularly Sister Rahel, as this is well outside of her duties."

"Has Sister Rahel agreed to care for the baby in her own time?" I ask.

"Yes, but it is not part of her paid duties," he explains, as if I was a simpleton. "The orphanage is ready to take the baby. The police can collect it to take it there at any time. It is taking up a space on the ward."

I wish we were doing this in Amharic. I'd feel less patronised. I think of switching, since, like Tadesse, I am fluent in either language, but it would seem petulant. Instead, I speak slowly and deliberately back, trying to keep the ire from my voice.

"It was my understanding that both Mariam and Rahel were carrying out these extra duties voluntarily, and that the baby's continued place on the ward was authorised by you. Is that not the case?"

"I said the baby could stay," Tadesse's eyes are bright now and he is smiling manically, "but I never agreed to these... details. I regret giving Mariam my initial permission. She should have discussed her plans explicitly with me before proceeding because I would not have permitted it. The baby is on our ward, yet she is receiving care not stipulated for all babies. There have been other abandoned babies, many, in the past and yet—"

"It was my understanding, Dr Tadesse, that this was a test case, and as such an instructional experiment for the other staff. It may act as a spur to women to do kangaroo care, and also encourage mothers of sick babies to pump their milk. The baby's current gestational age is, what, thirty-seven weeks. Am I right?"

"Thirty-seven weeks and two days," he says checking his notes.

"All right. So I feel that this is a conversation that can wait a little longer. Please make space for her. Your points have been noted, Dr Tadesse."

He purses his lips, but says nothing. He'll be back. And it's not just Tadesse who Mariam will need to watch out for. I can see he has garnered the support of many of our colleagues. If I am completely honest with myself, I am beginning to doubt my professional judgement on the issue of the baby. Is it for Mariam, for the child or for some other unspecified principle that I have made this decision? I need to get out of this snake pit.

I'm just rising to leave when, unannounced, Dr Zelalem, the CEO, sweeps in with his escort of administrators. To what do we owe his presence? There is confusion. His arrival doesn't bode well. We sit to attention; some, like Tadesse, stand like naughty boys.

I've known Zelalem since I arrived in Ethiopia. He's the same age as me; I'm not sure which of us has aged better. He has more hair than me, certainly. His hairstyle, which always reminds me of the foam head of a microphone, is right out of the eighties. It's a statement that informs you his mind is on higher things than keeping up with fashion. He's become paunchy as he's aged; his round belly allows you to see his vest through the front buttons of his shirt. I don't envy him his job. I remember him when he was approachable, active on the ward, with words for the patients as well as the student doctors. We used to drink beer together in the *tella bets* of Kazanchis. Now he only speaks to a select coterie of staff, and he is feared or loathed by all. This is the price he's paid.

As a doctor, I respected him. I still respect him for taking on the poisoned chalice that is St George's Hospital, though I don't always agree with his decisions. Still, he's walking a tough line. There's an unwritten expectation that doctors' hospital work needs to be juggled with their private practice. One change of policy too far, one single reforming move that disrupts that balance, and the whole hospital would cry corruption. They'd stab him in the back before they'd see things change.

Does he know about the missing dialysis machine? The expensive donation that 'walked' out of the hospital by itself and was found for sale in Merkato with a hospital label still attached? Of course he does. But to claim it back he'd have to declare it stolen, and that would mean the doctors, nurses, porters and guards who helped it walk down seven flights of stairs would have to be challenged. The hospital is operated by a private mafia who have them all by the balls. Sometimes I think the only thing to be done is to sack everyone, rip down the buildings and start again.

Zelalem is in a hurry. He isn't even going to sit down. Instead he stands in front of us, delivering his message with disdain.

"Complaints have been made," he begins, accusingly, scanning around the room for culprits, "about the condition of the labour ward." We all hold his gaze unfalteringly. "Politically motivated complaints, complaints seeking to undermine the current administration, have been made to the ministry." He pauses, as if expecting someone to come forward and admit guilt. No one does.

"As a result, until further notice, the ministry is closing the labour ward with immediate effect. All midwives will be reassigned to other hospitals while crucial structural and engineering work is done."

The news is a shock. My first thought is Mariam. What will she do? Where will she go? Back to England? She's due to leave soon, I know, but this soon? I am confused by my reaction. Of course it's none of my business what she decides to do. I made a decision not to get involved, to stay professional. Zelalem is still talking, but for a few moments I have not taken in anything he has said.

"I will be conducting an investigation as to the source of these complaints. When the investigation is completed," the CEO says pointedly, "there will be discussions about which staff will be invited back to work at the hospital. Those of you who work on the labour ward, please remain to discuss the matter; the rest, please go about your business."

There is a low mutter of apprehension. We who work in the NICU stand, leaving an unfortunate few to an uncomfortable interrogation. The conditions have deteriorated pretty badly these past few years. It's good news that something is going to be done. I wonder who the whistle-blower was. I hope it wasn't Mariam. Tadesse is hovering around the CEO trying to catch his eye. He has a nervous smile on his face that is pissing me off. Zelalem finally clocks Tadesse, nods and scans the room. When the big boss sees me, he pauses, as if he is about to speak, and I know Tadesse has had his ear about Mariam's baby.

"John," he says tersely.

"Yes?"

But he does not continue. Maybe there's something from our past he remembers, or maybe he's just too tired for another fight. He pinches the bridge of his nose and looks down.

"Another time," he says, waving me away.

I get out of the room quickly. I don't want to be in there

a moment longer than I have to. I know Zelalem and I know that thanks to Dr Tadesse, my card has been marked. I need to find Mariam and tell her the news about the ward. If it means she's leaving sooner than I thought, so be it. I would just like to know.

In the corridor my phone buzzes a text message against my thigh.

Hi bro. Just to let you know that Emma had the baby last night. Big, healthy girl. 8lbs, 3oz. Andrea Rose. Speak to you soon. Barns.

I breathe out, a warm rush of guilt and love for my little brother and his kind wife. A niece. Andrea Rose. Along the corridor, Baby X, Merkato lies in her crib, her fate dependent on the kindness of strangers. It's a funny old game.

Mariam

The grey light of dawn. I am half dreaming. A long-forgotten memory of the orphanage.

I am sitting in the shade behind a white building, digging in the damp cool soil with a stick. There is a particular quality to the red Sidama earth. The rich clay is shot through with tiny granules of sand that sparkle. I must have eaten some of the soil, because I can taste it, mineral, iron-rich and scratchy on my tongue. I scrape the stick through a groove in the soil, enjoying the slick crease I am engraving. It is chilly in the shade of the *enset* grove that surrounds the building, and a breeze riffles through the false banana leaves, but the feeling of the still warm shit in my cloth wraps is comforting. I can smell it, foul, but familiar. They will be angry when they find out, but the comfort of the warmth, the owning of the shit outweighs the thrill of panic.

I am so engrossed in digging my hole that I don't hear her coming. She calls me by my name but I hear only sound, like that of an animal bleating or barking. She makes the sound many times but I want to dig. I have the idea that I will make an impression in the soil that is the size of my body and slot myself into it. Not a grave, but a kind of packaging, like the kind the cheap imitation Barbie I was once given came in. The plastic vacuum-moulded to her skin. She looked so comfortable and contained. I want to feel the cool packed earth around me, firm and fitting. When I am done, I will lie there all day. But she comes and I am prodded. She takes my arm and hauls me away to light and noise and self-forgetting and I am bereft. I howl noiselessly into my pillow.

I wake and lie for several moments holding my breath. My arm is numb where I have been lying on it. The trigger for the dream. I feel such loss; for what? A hole in the ground? I cannot even tell if this is a real memory or an imagined one. There are no records. No witness. No imprint in the soil.

According to my adoptive mother, I was a year old when I came to the orphanage. I was adopted out of the orphanage when I was nearly three. When my mother and father took me, they had only seen pictures. All they knew was that I was a female. I could not speak or walk unaided. It was predicted that I would never do either, and that I might always be incontinent. I was prone to flailing tantrums that some suggested might be fits. They still wanted me. "Why?" I asked my mother, one of the rare times we spoke of it. "Because you needed loving." But why me? Why not another child? "You were the child allocated to us. We didn't choose you, no more than we could have chosen a birth child. You were given to us." It wasn't enough. I wanted her to say that they'd seen something special in my face, a light in my eyes. That they had wanted me for me alone.

They came to Addis Ababa to collect me. They stayed a week. Did they not have second thoughts when they saw me? "No." But I couldn't speak. I screamed and bit when they tried to change me. I had ringworm on my head. I had to be carried because I wouldn't walk. "No. We were scared, but you were more scared than us. And we knew we could give you a chance."

I lie in bed and stare at the ceiling. A long shaft of golden light probes between the crack in the curtain. I feel bleak. I never think of the orphanage, but sometimes it forces its way in, dark and dangerous and unresolved. Sunlight in reverse.

I used to long to be alone. The sounds of the orphanage were clanking metal plates, wailing, screeching. The sounds filled up my head, blurring the edges of things. The scorch of hunger; at least it was mine. It reminded me of my body.

The memories don't have words attached to them. They say I didn't speak, but I must have understood some Sidamic, or perhaps some Amharic. I can't sift the memories, I can only let them wash, wailing over me. As a child, I used to bang my head on the wall. Perhaps I should do that now.

I haven't been to the orphanage in Addis Ababa, the one that the baby will be sent to. I have gone out of my way to block my ears to stories of it. A few have crept in regardless. Rahel talks about the lack of staff. The damp mattresses. She says they prop the older babies' bottles because they have no time to feed them. It's not their fault. There are too many babies. Not enough staff. The babies are mostly girls, and the physically and mentally handicapped. Most mornings a new baby is left outside the gate and its mother never found.

When I banged my head against the wall, I was looking for my mother's face, but I don't want to know her face now. It would ruin everything. Lying in bed, a grown woman, I become a brooding teenager when I think of my birth mother. How could she have left me? How could she? I don't want to have to imagine her reasons, I don't want to be understanding about how hard her circumstances must have been; the hurt is too hard. For her youth, for her poverty, for her desperation, I could forgive T'irunesh, but I cannot forgive my mother for abandoning me. I block out her face and the imagining of her life in the same way she must have done to me. Does she ever wonder if I survived? Where I am now? Don't think of it! I turn and bury my face in my pillow. I run through all the things I have to do today, dragging myself into the world of errands and tasks and practicalities. Coping strategies, that's what they're called. I cope.

There are two kinds of midwife. There are the jobbers who catch babies and the other kind, the Ina Mays, the placenta-smoothie-making, lotus-birth, hippy-shit kind. I am the former. If the mother wants to listen to whale music, that's her deal; I'll help her get the baby out with the minimum of hassle, but if it goes wrong, I'm not going to be there to help her make sense of it all. Sorry. It's not me. Not the way I do things. Sometimes things don't go right. You can only do what you can do. When it comes down to it, if the worst happens, you just have to survive.

So I will go to the hospital and help. I will put in my hours with the baby, and give her a chance of survival. You can only do so much.

And yet... For her, the baby, I want more than survival. I want her to be happy. To grow up free from fear and without the black holes of misery and forgetting that riddle my past. The moment I admit this to myself the holes in me open and billow wide and I am nothing but black emptiness once more. This is what she does to me. She makes me vulnerable and it is killing me. She makes me want to love her.

So I will set limits. I cannot be soft-skinned. Perhaps I am hard, like Betty said. A hard bitch. Perhaps I will never let anyone get really close to me, really see me. Instead of a hole in the ground, I have built myself a shell. So I will never have children. So what? Plenty of people get by without those things. It's a trade-off.

I get out of bed and stand before the curtains. I fix my smile. The sunlight pours in.

The baby

The rhythms of the feeds make up her day. She has learned to lap like a cat from a cup. A look of intense concentration comes across her small face as she feeds. There is nothing more important. The nurses have been taught not to tip the milk into her. She must take it herself and the muscles in her tongue are developing as a result. Still she has made no sound. She is a silent child; all she needs to express she communicates with her long fingers, the arch of her still furry back, and the furrow of her sparse brow. Her limbs ache from lying all day; she cannot move her own body to roll or change position because the nerves required have not connected. It will be three months at least before she can turn onto her stomach. The programme of development cannot be sped up, only disrupted by misadventure. The sweet taste of the milk takes away some of the pain from lying on her back all day. And the relief of being held, of no longer retaining her own boundaries but being defined by someone else. She should be moving, mobile, carried. Somewhere, out there in the world, her mother is moving about.

They swaddle her arms next to her sides because, quite without volition, they writhe and turn, grasping with her tiny brown nails as if searching for fur and branches. Once she spilled a whole cup of milk. She has never met the woman who provides the milk, but in it she tastes the spices she uses in her cooking, every day a different flavour to experience and explore. The nurses handle the milk with suspicion; they believe a mother's milk is good for her baby, but there is something uncomfortable about this expressed bodily fluid. It is like the difference between the saliva in your mouth and a spit in your palm; one is intimate, the other exposed, contaminated. They wear gloves and wrinkle their noses when they feed the child who, despite all odds, is thriving.

Beyond the rhythms of her stomach and her bowel, there is the rhythm of the ward and the passage of the sun. At 5.30 the sun begins to rise over Roosevelt, but it is not until 7 a.m. that the sun is high enough to challenge the dim electric lights of the ward. The gauzy curtains block the blinding rays, but the baby senses the change in light. She has begun to associate it with the first feed of the day. The nurses are more patient at this time; the shift has changed, and they have had their breakfast. They hold her in a business-like way while she does her serious lapping. After her feed, she may squit; tiny smears of yellow milk in her enormous nappy. They wipe between her thin buttocks before sliding her into her incubator. She hears the sounds of the breakfast trolley. The clanks echo in her bones; she tastes the metallic noise. Later come the ward round visits; she is handled and protests; each unexpected touch is like fire; flashes of light shiver up and down her nerves like the light through some primitive underwater creature; she is soft-skinned, unprotected. Her heart pitter-patters with the flood of adrenaline and it is several hours before she is able to stop grimacing. Yet while she cannot predict, her body remembers, and each time, she feels a little less stress. Her brain is growing. The milk is laying down the myelin sheath. She is more resilient.

She is growing within and without; inside her lungs, her alveoli are dividing and expanding. Already her ovaries contain all of the eggs she will ever secrete, all her future children. Inside her gut, fingers of villi lengthen and ripple, extending to absorb the nutrients she needs to grow.

There is noise. A tone she recognises, but with an anxiety in it that makes her hold her breath.

"She's not ready."

"We don't have room."

"Yes. There's room. Dr Tadesse, please. She's so small."

"We have other babies coming in all the time. Sicker than her."

"Then let them share the incubator. Don't send her yet. She's not ready. She was so small for dates. You gave me permission. I was given permission. John, Dr Spencer, gave me permission. At least until she's term."

"And I am telling you that this hospital is not a boarding house for you to extend her stay according to your fancies. I am coming to the end of my patience with your project."

"Please, Tadesse."

"Sister Mariam, I am not in the habit of raising voices over the beds of babies on this ward! It is not dignified."

"But you promised!"

"I... Well, have it your way. From what I hear, you may not be here much longer to care for the child anyway."

"What do you mean by that?"

"You'll find out soon enough. When the proper announcements are made."

There is a pause and the lid of the incubator is roughly opened. A warm bundle is placed next to her. She smells amniotic fluid, familiar, warm, comforting. She turns her face towards the baby, mouthing. The baby is still; he was born blue and floppy. Only his pinched face can be seen within his blanket. It will be some time before they know the outcome. His mother is being stitched in another hospital. The baby has extricated her arms from the swaddling and she moves her long fingers, making them ripple in the warm air.

Some time later that afternoon the boy baby is taken away to his mother. She is unsettled. The familiar voice tells her she is about to be lifted. She braces her body against the sound and the anticipated movement. She is unwrapped and slid next to pliable skin. The skin is tacky, elastic after the sensation of the bed sheets. Warmth, the throb of blood pumping beneath the ribs. But she cannot relax.

The body that holds her is tight, hard. It does not absorb her, only hosts her. The tension and the chemicals begin to affect her. Animal-like, she can smell the cortisol in the thin film of sweat on the chest on which she rests. It is dirty stuff, waste. A poison message. She wriggles, trying to move. A large hand cups her body.

"What's the matter?"

She feels the vibration in the top of her head, through her open fontanelle. The voice is trapped at the throat; there is no corresponding vibration in the stomach to tell her that the sentiment is meant. She squirms. The body tightens and the throb of blood speeds up. The blanket is lifted and she is examined for aggravating causes; none are found and the blanket is returned. She finds it unbearable to be held by this person today. She feels a tension in her chest and opens her tiny mouth. The small strangled cry she makes surprises her. It is the first sound she has ever made.

The person who holds her gasps, and the baby feels a deep muscle that was clenched in the woman's diaphragm spasm. The woman reaches inside her top and removes the baby; she holds her gently in one hand, supporting her head with the other.

"What is it?" she says.

The woman looks anxiously at the child's face. The baby opens her dark, wondering eyes and sees the woman start at the reflection those eyes give back to her. But she cannot lie. She flinches. Her small body is appalled. The woman's panic, her insouciant efficiency, the shallowness of her actions make her recoil. She squeezes her eyes shut once more. The woman holds her briefly at arms' length, as if deciding what to do.

She feels the heat of the woman's flush and scents the rush of protective hormones. She is pulled back to the woman's chest and rocked. At first the baby tenses, but then she senses the woman's release, and a new tenderness. Against her small feet she feels a new softness in the woman's belly. The baby unclenches. Simultaneously, their heartbeats slow and their breath comes more easily.

The woman rocks and rocks and rocks, whispering. "Hey, hey. It's all right. It's going to be all right."

After some time, the baby wakes from a deep sleep to hear women whispering. The whispering would once have rasped through her spinal column. Now she hears it with her ears, intrigued by the urgency.

"Mariam. Have you heard? They are shutting the labour ward!"

"Rahel, don't joke me."

The woman sits up sharply, and the baby is jolted.

"No, it's true. They are renovating the labour ward.

Rewiring the electricity. Fixing the pipes. A notice has just gone up."

The woman emits a low whistle. The chest beneath the baby's ear reverberates with soft sound.

"So that's what Tadesse was hinting at. Well, that's wonderful. It's exactly what's needed."

"Yes, but what about you? What about your job?"

"Good question. I'll have to talk to VSO, but, well, I'm coming to the end of my contract so it's too late to be assigned anywhere else. So, I suppose, I'll come here. Be here, with this little one. If they'll still let me."

The baby squirms. She does not feel secure.

"I have to go. I'll be back later for my shift with the baby. I just wanted to tell you. I'm so sorry, Mariam."

When the woman has gone, the hands stroke the blanket that covers her back. But she cannot yield to them and drift into sleep; there is tension in the woman's body and her heartbeat races. She feels the woman stir and sit up. The blanket is pulled and tucked tight across the baby's back.

"Hello, John."

"Hi." A low rumble. This time the voice is quieter. It does not sound too close.

She could drift back into sleep.

"How is the patient?"

"She's doing well. She's gained 125 grams this week. Her breathing has been steady and there have been no tachycardic episodes for three weeks."

"That's wonderful. You must be very pleased."

"Of course."

The baby waits for the voices to continue but there is silence. She can hear the woman's heart sluicing blood. It is unsettling, this mismatch between body and voice.

"You've heard about the labour ward?"

"Yes. Just now. At least it's finally getting the refurbishment it needs."

"What will you do? Will you leave?"

"I... I have no plans to. I'll stay until my visa expires."

"Right."

There follows a long silence during which the woman's breathing is shallow, erratic. The baby squirms.

"God knows what the ministry said to Zelalem. He's furious. I wouldn't want to be in their shoes if he finds out who the whistle-blower was. Mariam, it wasn't you, was it?"

"No! Of course not. I kind of wish I'd thought of it, though."

There is another long silence.

"Listen, I have to go back to the UK for a few days," the woman says. "I'm on an interview panel to recruit for the new head of postnatal ward. Will you see she's looked after while I'm gone?"

"I'll do my best. Rahel will stand in for you though, won't she?"

"Yes, but Rahel has no say in her care. Don't let Tadesse—"

"Mariam, you know the hierarchy. He's the senior neonatologist. If he decides she's going, there won't be much I can do about it."

"Use your influence. Ring me if anything happens. She's not ready to go to the orphanage yet."

"But she will go. Eventually. How do you feel about that?"

"What can I say? I hope she finds someone to love her. In a parallel universe..."

"I'll do my best to see she's well looked after."

The baby hears the man inhale. He coughs.

"My sister, Lidet, is cooking lunch for me today. She lives nearby. Do you want to join us?"

"John, I..." There is confusion and surprise in her voice.

The baby stops breathing in response to the woman's breath.

"I'd like you to. Would you?"

"OK."

When the woman starts breathing again, the baby releases her own breath in a long yawn, stretches her tiny fists as if in jubilation and then lets out a tiny triumphant fart. The woman shakes silently. The man laughs softly before moving away.

"I'll come and find you later," he says.

Mariam

John drives me from the hospital in his knackered white Land Cruiser. I watch his freckled hands on the wheel. A line from that Radiohead song I used to like comes into my head, something about skin and angels, and my chest constricts with wanting him. What the hell I am doing, saying yes to another date with him, opening all this up again? In a few months I'll be gone, and anyway, he turned me down. Quite emphatically. Why is he asking me out again? Is this an attempt to establish some kind of sexless friendship, to salve his guilt, or is he having second thoughts? I can hardly believe how passively I'm accepting this. Back in London I'd have made him throw his cards on the table; a straight choice, either you want me or you don't. It's not that difficult.

He drives well, weaving though the traffic, giving way to the pedestrians on Churchill and earning small waves and smiles in the process. We swing round Sebastopol. The great gun's replica has a naked man lying spread-eagled on it, sunning himself. Not what the emperor imagined.

Lidet lives near Piazza, the old Italian quarter of Addis Ababa. He parks in a back street, and engages a small boy to guard his car for a few birr.

"Here's hoping my wing mirrors are still here when we get back." He grins rakishly.

I should leave now before I humiliate myself, I think, but he is already knocking on the compound gate.

"Ene negn!" It's me! The family guard lets us in, pulling John to his shoulder in an embrace.

Lidet's house is lovely. It's built back into the hillside, shaded by eucalyptus trees with a small garden of pomegranate and orange trees. It must have been built by Italians, because high above my head is the kind of balcony Juliet could sigh to her Ethiopian Romeo from. I feel shy. I want to know who I am. A friend or a prospective lover? Sod it. They'll have to take me as they find me.

Lidet comes to the door in her apron. John is right. She's extremely pretty. She's late thirties, maybe a little older than me, tall, with a fine long nose, full lips and warm curves. She has the most luscious, luminous skin and the kind of heavy-lidded eyes that make her look like she plotting something. Her hair is tied back into a black headscarf that gathers at the nape of her neck. She opens her arms to her brother and I find myself scanning to see if there are any signs of unfilial attraction from either side. But they just seem loving. She holds his face in her hands and touches her cheek to his three times. His hands are at her waist and shoulder, but he is already looking past her into the house.

"Are Belai and Emnet here today?" he asks in Amharic.

She nods, and before I have a chance to introduce myself two kids charge out of the house and throw themselves at John. The ten-year-old boy and the plump seven-year-old girl in a sparkly party dress hug him round the middle, grinning at me and staring with big eyes. John calls over in English, "Lidet, this is Mariam."

Lidet comes to me and I too am pulled into an embrace.

"How are you?" she asks, in clear English. "It's such a pleasure to meet you," she says, with emphasis.

I glance at John, but he is busying himself with the

children. I wonder whether he has said something about me to her? He is extracting sweets from his pocket, in a most unpaediatrician-like fashion. She draws me inside, to a bright dining room, laid with many places. There are staged family photos on the wall, featuring the Ethiopian family members. But John is in all the casual photos on the mantelpiece. I saunter over for a look. A young John with curly, floppy hair stands between a serious older couple.

"My father and mother. They will join us for lunch," Lidet says. "You'll have to speak a little loud for them, they are getting old. We're having *doro wot*. I hope you like Ethiopian food. Of course you do, you are Ethiopian."

"Well, not really," I begin, but she laughs and puts her hand on my shoulder and I see she means it as a form of acceptance, the way John is Ethiopian to her. So I accept. I try to follow her into the kitchen to help stir the bubbling vat of oily red *wot*, but she shoos me out and tells me to keep John company. There is a small smile on her lips that worries me; is she deceived about our relationship? That's all I need, having to play the doting girlfriend to a man who wants to keep me at arm's length.

John is sitting with the kids on the front steps in the sun. He'll burn if he stays there, I find myself thinking protectively. The boy, Belai, is on his lap telling him a long enthusiastic story in Amharic, while the girl, Emnet, appears to be going through his hair for nits.

"She's counting my freckles," he explains, somewhat embarrassed. "To see if I have any more since she last saw me. You wouldn't believe how envious they are."

He reaches round and pulls Emnet onto his lap, shunting Belai off. Dramatically he examines her face, neck and ears. "Any freckles here? No? Surely just one? Maybe we should call the doctor. Oh, hang on, I am the doctor." The girl squeals and wriggles.

I laugh.

"Are you *Habesha*?" Emnet asks me from John's lap in Amharic.

"Emnet!" John shushes.

"No, it's OK," I tell him. In my bad Amharic, I try to explain. "I was born in Ethiopia, so yes, I am East African, *Habesha*, but when I was a little girl I went to live with my new mum and dad in England."

"Oh, so you're *adopted*," says Emnet seriously.

John looks embarrassed; I am amused at his discomfort. He changes the subject.

"Emnet, will you show Mariam where to wash her hands before lunch?"

The little girl sighs dramatically, but takes my hand and leads me to a small outhouse where I carefully wash my hands. I catch my face in the mirror. I look terrified. I bite my lips to get some colour in them and push some errant curls back in place. I wish I'd had time to go back and change. I am wearing casual slacks and an old cotton shirt that smells of the hospital. I remember Betty questioning me about John and I feel like I am about to be presented to my future in-laws. I scowl and feel irritated with him for putting me in this position. Then I take a breath and remember that I am a guest, and an ambassador for my country, and that everyone is trying very hard. I should make the effort to charm them, no matter who they think I am.

When I get back to the dining room, John's 'parents' are there. They are delightful. They are little and old, his mother dressed in a white *shama* with her hair plaited in Tigray style. His dad heaves himself to his feet and clasps my hand. He's a handsome man in his seventies, wiry and bright-eyed. I bet he still holds the floor with his *eskista* dancing at family gatherings. They speak broken English, but it's enough to get by. Better than my Amharic. John is fluent and he keeps up a running banter with everyone. I have never seen him so animated. He looks younger, more playful. I want to pull him into a side room and kiss him, to make him feel as flustered as I do. Does he not feel the heavy tension between us? When we speak, it feels like time has slowed to a crawl, that every word is laden, every glance full of meaning. Or am I imagining that? Is he going to keep wrong-footing me like this?

We sit down to eat. I am seated next to John, and when he puts his hand on the small of my back to guide me to my place I almost leap into the air; he seems oblivious. I try to catch his eye, but he is avoiding mine. Lidet brings though the big bowl of *doro wot;* boiled eggs, glistening with spicy red oil, float temptingly among meaty pieces of chicken. There are several plates of spongy *injera*, sliced into neat rolls. There's *aib,* a fluffy cottage cheese that you eat with rich spinach *wot*, and a mouth-watering potato-and-carrot stew. There's a big bowl of thick *miser wot*, a fiery lentil stew, and a delicious mixture of beetroot with green beans. I still have to concentrate on not using my left hand to eat. They are so adept at eating with their right hand, ripping the *injera* into little pads and scooping up the *wot*. John's mother reaches over to him and pops a little handful into his mouth, which he receives with a nod. It's called *gursha*; feeding the ones you love by hand shows a special bond. John reaches over to take a plate of *wot* and the hairs on his arm brush my skin; tiny stippled goosebumps prickle its surface. My breath is shaky. I want him, God I want him, but I am angry with him for making me feel so exposed.

"Mariam has been in Ethiopia for nearly two years. She works as a midwife at St George's."

"She's *Habesha*," pipes up Emnet through a mouthful of *injera*.

"And how do you like Ethiopia?" asks John's father.

"I *love* Ethiopia," I say, and am surprised by the force of my response. It silences the gathering for a moment. Then we laugh.

"I like it very much. Everyone is very kind. It is a beautiful country. "

"But unfortunately, Mariam won't be with us for much longer," John says.

I turn to John surprised. Is he making it clear that I'm not a prospective daughter-in-law then? His face is unreadable.

"That's a shame. We hope you will return many times. You are always welcome here," continues his mother.

"Thank you," I say. I begin to relax, but I feel faintly disappointed. I like them. I like the idea of being part of their gang. "I hope I will be back often," I say. This country has crept under my skin. Its proud, loving, distrustful people, with their wide smiles and suspicious eyes; I share their genes but not their stories.

"I am sure we'll find some work for you to do when you come back to visit. There are always babies being born, after all," says John. He sounds rueful.

Lidet laughs.

"This one seems to find work wherever he goes. Even on a Sunday he is at the hospital when he should be at church. In some ways, you will never be *Habesha*, John..."

He grins and shrugs.

"But if he hadn't been so in love with his work, perhaps I

would not be here today. So I cannot complain."

"He told me he met you when you were sick with TB," I say.

"She would have died," says Lidet's mother. "She was going to die. The angels had called her. We had tried everything and there was nothing more we could do. I could not even cry any more. Do you remember? My eyes were dry from crying."

"She is our only child. To see your child dying before you is a terrible thing. Then God sent this man to us," says the father.

"No," says John.

"Yes. When he came into the room with his yellow hair, my wife turned to me and said the Angel Raphael has come," the old man laughs. "And sure enough you did not leave my daughter until she was well again."

John puts his hand on the Ethiopian's shoulder and squeezes it.

"They told us there was nothing they could do, but in three weeks of his care the coughing and the fever stopped and she started to get better. And he was always there. And when he was not there he was talking to people for her, to get medicine. We give our thanks to this man," the old man says simply. "He is my son."

John looks embarrassed. Lidet leans over and places her hand over his. I feel a stab of envy as she slides her fingers between his freckled knuckles.

"But we saved John too, no?" she says, laying her head on his shoulder.

John looks at her, confused.

"If it weren't for us, you'd still be travelling around the world looking for somewhere to call home. Do you remember the pineapple?"

"Ah, the pineapple..." says John with a smile. It seems to be a family in-joke.

"The pineapple?" I enquire after a few moments. Whatever the pineapple was it seems symbolic. They are all trying to stifle laughter now.

"Lidet loves pineapple," says John's mother eventually. She looks sly at the memory. "When she started to get better, I brought a pineapple to the hospital for her. To celebrate. A nice big ripe one it was, all cut up into pieces. John was there in his white coat. I asked him to share some with us, but he said no. This young doctor, all pale and full of study. It was an insult. He would not let us thank him, even in this small way. I said you *must* have some pineapple. Still he said, 'No. I shouldn't. I am working.'"

His mother draws herself up in indignation at the memory and I laugh. She continues.

"Those other patients can wait, I said. You *will* eat some pineapple with us." She pauses for effect. "Mariam, when I decide something, there is no point in disagreeing. Did you eat the pineapple, John?"

"I did," he admits.

"How much pineapple did you eat?" she teases.

"I ate the whole pineapple."

"The whole thing?" I exclaim.

"She's a formidable woman."

The whole family guffaw. Clearly the old lady is not to be messed with.

John's embarrassed but he is smiling.

"Lidet was a patient. I didn't think I should cross the line, be too friendly, get too familiar," he tells me in defence.

John's mother scoffs.

"He saved her life, brought my daughter's soul back from the hands of the angels, but he wouldn't eat my pineapple," she says disgustedly. This makes Lidet hoot with laughter, but her mother shushes her. "Bodies have people living in them. Sometimes you doctors forget that. It was good pineapple, wasn't it? Sweet. That was when he started to become my son."

He cannot meet her eye, but bows his head. Lidet breaks the moment.

"So, Mariam. Guess what we are having for dessert! I hope you like pineapple," she laughs.

"I love pineapple!"

"Good! Don't worry, we won't make you eat a whole one!"

She starts to clear the plates and I try to help but I am instructed to stay where I am. While the others chat in Amharic I turn to John.

"So you stayed in Ethiopia for the pineapple," I joke.

"Well, that was the start. And then I couldn't leave, because..." He looks a bit lost.

"Because?" I ask.

"Because I needed to know the end of the story." He is looking at me, with those pale blue eyes, and briefly I think I might pass out. And then Lidet brings in bowls of pineapple and the family is talking and laughing and eating dessert as if nothing had been said.

He drives me home. I don't ask him in for coffee, but he gets out of his car to show me to my door.

"I'll be away for a week. Please make sure she's OK," I say.

"The baby? Of course. Mariam, this time it's only a week. How will it be when you have to give her up for good?"

"I don't know. I don't want to think about it."

"You need to think about it. You will get hurt."

"I'll be OK."

He thrusts his hands into his pockets and looks at his feet. I am not going to ask him in. It's his turn. I need him to be clearer with me.

"Thank you for meeting my family."

"I liked them very much."

"And they you. And me too..."

I am suddenly furious with him.

"John. This isn't fair. You said—"

"I know. I thought... Listen, I thought it would save us both a lot of pain if... but I don't want you to go. Can't you stay a while longer?"

I can't believe he is asking me this. But his face is serious, practical.

"You could get a job here. Not for me, but to see if... well, partly for me."

"But I hardly know you. And what about my job in England?"

"I know, I know." He is humiliated. "It doesn't make sense, does it? It's risky, but look, I think it's worth the risk. It might be worth it. *We* might. I will understand if you don't, if you can't, but... Bloody hell. Ignore me, Mariam. It's been a long time. I'm not good at this. I should learn to take no for an answer."

"No, I'm not, I'm not turning you down, I want..."

I place my hand on his arm and feel the spring of hair under my palm. His hand slides round my waist and I step closer. Slowly, as if I were sleeping and he dare not wake me, he quietly lays his lips against mine. I close my eyes and breathe him in. His lips are cool, dry, and I feel the scratch of stubble. The kiss was brief, experimental. We stand close. I move my mouth softly to his and feel him inhale me. He smells of cotton and sunshine. He is a good man and he wants me. Why is it so difficult?

"I'll be back in a week," I tell him, tracing a freckle on his cheek with my finger, then running it over his blond eyebrow. He turns to my touch, butting my hand with his forehead and kissing my palm. "Can you wait?"

"I'll have to," he smiles ruefully.

As he drives away on the other side of the door I hug myself and laugh through my fear. What have we done?

Tewodros

It starts when one of them pushes him aside. He makes his body leaden, woollen, absorbs the sharp action like a sudden noise. The glue-sniffers are back, their light heads scrambled with solvent fumes, high and speeding, flying. This time they are mean. They turn on him and begin to question him:

"Why are you here? Why don't you wash? Look at your hair – you look like a woman! You crazy shit, why don't you crawl off into the gutter and stay there?"

Always questioning. Never listening. No matter. The fits are coming daily now and he is too rapt in wonder, too exhausted to fight. When they realise what mysteries he has to impart, then they will shut their dirty mouths and listen. Then the police will put down their batons and beat him no more. There will come a time. Until then, until he has an audience with ears to hear, and wisdom to understand, he will guard his secrets. It will not be long now.

The glue-sniffers mock him. He lets their words bounce off him. He will not add these words to his list. They are not beautiful. Just commonplace words. But then, these boys are commoners. Inside he draws himself up, scathing; he is careful not to let his superiority show lest they guess who he is. Lest they glimpse his majesty. But there is no light of recognition in their widened pupils. They have shaved the sides of their heads, leaving a quiff on top. He would like to ask them where they got it done, he admires the daring parrot-like quirk of it. A man should express himself. But he dislikes the fact they are a gang. Gangs have never appealed to him; he cannot get the rules right.

They begin to shove him, ricocheting him back and forth within their triangle. He keeps his eyes low and grips onto his bag. A blow catches him in the stomach and he doubles over in pain. Hands push him down by the shoulders and he falls, curling himself protectively. The kicks come then, not hard, because the boys are only wearing flip-flops, but well aimed. A long toenail scores flesh from his cheek. There is suddenly spit on the ground; they are spitting on him. He feels warm liquid slide into one ear.

He makes himself retreat then; his hand goes to his face, to that place on his nose that offers sanctuary. He rubs to the sound of their panting and laughter. The stars begin to glimmer in a darkening sky.

A sense of freedom sweeps into him. He is at the bottom of the great Amba Meqdella. He understands now why some worship him, why some revile him for he is not quite of this world. He has the emperor in him.

His subjects are climbing hand over hand up the mountain, pushing packs of laden donkeys up the steep winding slopes. They are ascending to seek refuge, refuge from the great battle that is surely coming. They struggle, weary, up the slope, but he finds he floats above it. No one remarks on this, but it is incredible and pleasing to him. He hovers just over the surface of the ground, sweeping up the slope at a pace that outstrips his followers. As he moves he feels the breeze flutter in his sparkling white *shama*, and feels the long cotton robes about him move. He is a magnificent sight. He is a kingly sight. The peasants bow before him. They prostrate themselves in the mud at Tewodros's passing, but he gazes benevolently at them.

He can be brutal; he is father to this mountain nation and what father does not sometimes need to chastise his errant children? But he can be magnanimous too. His eyes chance upon the faces of the three glue-sniffing boys clinging together in fear and guilt, their parrot hair deflated now, greasy, and their drug-corroded brains scrabbling to engage with this sudden reversal. He pauses, lordly. He feels a great wash of responsibility overtake him. He puts out a hand to them. He sees it glows with the golden light of benediction. He places his palm on their greasy heads and one by one they faint with relief, with the unwarranted forgiveness. His followers applaud him; he turns, humbled, benign and bows to them, before sliding up the cliff face.

He feels the blast of chill air as he rises above the bluff. It takes his spirit, lifting it into the hard, blue sky, then delivers it back to him, clean. He sees the encampment they have prepared – the red velvet tents, the livestock enclosures. The view beneath stretches infinitely – yellow pastures, hazy distances. The iron brown of the mountains. All this belongs to him, to cherish or destroy as he sees fit.

He feels the red velvet of the tent flaps brush his cheeks as he slides into the dim interior. He is alone, standing in the antechamber of his destiny. At the back of the tent stands a tall mirror made of beaten brass, half swathed in curtains. He approaches. He must see what he has become, but he is afraid of facing disappointment. He puts out a hand, pushes the drapes aside, and looks deep into the emperor's eyes.

He is breathless. Transfixed. His heart is racing. He, the emperor, is all he imagined. A strong colt with a mane of tumbling hair. A hawk with fierce, clever eyes, set in a hard, handsome face. The emperor's spirit kindles in him, and he feels, sees, a smile curling on his proud lips.

He places one hand on the smooth cool brass.

"What must I do?"

"You must take a hostage," says the emperor. "Then they will listen."

Close, red velvet, and darkness. A sleep so deep that there are no pinpricks of light in the great night that now surrounds him.

When he wakes, he is lying in the street with congealed blood on one cheek, wet trousers, a splitting headache and an idea.

Dr Tadesse

Alemayehu Eshete is playing at Club Alize tonight and he cannot afford to be late. Eshete is the Ethiopian James Brown; he's been out of Ethiopia for years, lived in America during the Derg years, but now he's back and he plays regular slots at the jazz club. Tadesse loves the man with something approaching idolatry. He has all his CDs. In the past, his neighbours at the club have elbowed and shushed him when he's whooped too loud. But Eshete is a born performer – you can't help but be filled with joy as you watch him in the spotlight, shrugging his shoulders *eskista*-style while doing that little James Brown shoe shuffle. Tadesse shook him by the hand once after a gig and offered to buy him a drink. Eshete was polite, but tired. "Another time," he said. Maybe tonight they'd have the chance. If only Mariam's damn baby wasn't sick and taking up his time.

The child is febrile. Her body feels hot and when he lifts her out of the incubator she shows none of her usual signs of protest. She's limp. Her lips are dry and she's showing signs of dehydration. Sunken fontanelle. Scant urine. They have had to put a tube back in her arm, fluids and antibiotics. Tomorrow if she has not taken liquids orally they might put a tube back into her stomach through her nose to deliver some milk. If she makes it through the night.

It was only a matter of time. If she dies, Mariam will blame him, of course, he thinks angrily. So will the *ferenj* doctor, always so quick to jump to the midwife's defence. As a motherless child, the statistics were against the baby from the beginning. Infants are ten times more likely to die if their mother leaves or dies. He wonders how she got the infection. Could have been from anywhere, probably through one of the ward rounds, he thinks guiltily. Fifteen unhealthy students bringing their alien germs into the ward. Of course, you have to weigh up the value of those students getting to see real babies, the number of future lives saved by the learning experience. She was doing well. Everyone remarked on it. During the last ward round she had even opened her eyes and gazed at the trainee doctors. It was eerie. It was almost like she was looking for someone.

She started showing signs of a fever the following day, two days after Mariam left. Almost like she knew she'd gone. That's what the nurses said. Superstitious breed, nurses. Of course the baby didn't know. Mariam is no more a person to her than that little nurse, Rahel, who dutifully puts in those ridiculous shifts with her. Well, there will be no more of that now he is in charge. The baby is too sick. What if all the mothers of sick babies started putting them down their shirts and insisting on a comfy chair to incubate their own feverish offspring? It would be chaos. The baby will stay in its incubator and it is lucky even to have a place on the ward.

It's late, 10 p.m., and the night nurses are on duty. Time to finish up, and get a taxi down to Bole to watch the show. Eshete will be on in half an hour. Tadesse pictures him limbering up back stage, in his shiny black suit with his oiled hair. The ward's short-staffed as usual so he's had to write up some records and it's held him up. Outside it is chilly and the overnighting mothers have plugged the holes in the window frames with newspaper. The lights of Addis spread out beneath the window. He can remember when only a few lights pricked the darkness of the city at night, when whole blocks were plunged into black. Now there are streetlights up Roosevelt and every home has electricity. Apart from during power cuts. Thank God for the ancient hospital generator. When that goes, the hospital will be consigned to the Middle Ages.

The double doors swish open and shut. Another baby being admitted? That would really screw things up. He'll miss Eshete if it's an admission. But it's not. It's John. What's he doing here at this time of night?

"Tadesse. You still here?" He looks annoyed. But then he usually looks annoyed about something.

"You know how it is. The babies don't fix themselves. Why are you here?" Tadesse is suspicious. Is he being checked up on?

The foreign doctor looks uncomfortable.

"I came to take a look at Mariam's baby. I said I would keep an eye out for her while she's gone."

Tadesse barks a short laugh.

"The man-hours that that baby has taken. Are you off work now or is this hospital time?"

Dr John holds his gaze, steady, confrontational.

"I'm on my own time. How is she?"

"Everything is in hand," says the Ethiopian, pointedly returning to his notes.

"How is she?"

If he wants a fight, he can have one, but he is not missing his show.

"She's pyrexic," he replies perfunctorily, putting his pen down. "She has an infection. I've put her on an ampicillin drip. She'll be monitored through the night."

"Can I see her?" John asks.

The Ethiopian man shrugs.

"Help yourself," he says dismissively, but without being able to disguise the anger in his voice.

He watches surreptitiously through the glass as the British doctor examines the child. Doctor John. Such a good doctor, he sneers. So caring, so tender. He watches the man's high forehead furrow as he checks the baby. He's no fool. He knows the odds aren't in her favour. All these years, he's kept himself apart. Even those first years when they worked side by side in wards full of children with pneumonia, when they slept in their work clothes on the floor of the office. Hardly ever did he accept an invitation for drinks after work. Always has somewhere else to be. Keeps his private life so private you wonder what he's trying to hide. He wouldn't be surprised if the good doctor was one of those unnatural types who did it with other men. Then the hilarious thought strikes him that perhaps by showing a special interest in the child the pale doctor is trying to get into lovely Mariam's knickers. What a laugh! Well, stranger things have happened. Perhaps her English upbringing has perverted her taste so that she finds this ghost of a man attractive. In that case, she's welcome to him. He's given up trying to work out what makes her tick in any case. He looks forward to the day when she will be gone. Things will be simpler.

The doctor comes back, peeling off his gloves and flicking them into the waste bin.

"She's extremely ill," he says.

Thank you, doctor, thinks Tadesse, for sharing that gem of diagnosis.

"I should call Mariam. She would want to know."

"She has a job interview tomorrow, doesn't she? Better wait."

"Has Rahel been in today?"

The Ethiopian puts down his pen. It is 10.17. Eshete will be on stage in thirteen minutes. He will miss his first number.

"Yes. But we're short-staffed. She's needed for other duties."

"I thought she did the skin-to-skin after work."

"The baby is too sick to be skin-to-skin. I have forbidden it."

Dr John looks astonished.

"According to Mariam it is the skin-to-skin that has kept her alive until now."

"This is my ward, and I'm drawing a line under the unusual care of this baby. She should never have been made a special case. The care of sick children should be standardised. The other mothers will start to ask questions. That's my decision."

"It sounds political to me, Tadesse," says Dr John, with narrowed eyes.

"This whole hospital is political. The care of this baby has slipped under the radar of the administration so far, but it is not professional to have this *ferenji* come and start subverting things, not to mention paying for repairs that were none of her business."

"Oh, leave it with the toilets. This is all about the fact she's a *ferenji*."

"I can't have one baby treated differently."

"Even if it means saving her life?"

"Absolutely. Why should she live when others die?"

"Oh, so it's a philosophical point," sneers Dr John. "That's all right then. Listen, Tadesse, don't dress this up in big ideas. You don't like the fact that for all the medicine we've prescribed, a little thing like actually holding a baby might have made the most difference. Does it make you feel threatened?"

"I haven't got time for this conversation," Tadesse says, standing up abruptly. "I am not threatened by that baby, nor by Mariam, nor by you. I am the senior neonatologist on this ward and I make the decisions. Not you, not her. Now if you don't mind, I have to leave."

"And if you don't mind, I will stay with the baby for a few hours. Don't worry, I won't take her out of the incubator."

"I don't know why you're doing this, John."

"Because I was asked to."

"You should watch out for your professional reputation."

"Thank you for the warning," replies the Englishman. "Or was it a threat?"

Tadesse takes off his white coat and puts on his jacket.

As he does so, Dr John reads through the baby's notes and does not raise his head to say goodbye. The time is 10.22. With luck Tadesse will have time to catch the second half of Eshete's set, but first he needs a few Johnnie Walkers to calm his nerves and help him forget this whole unpleasant conversation.

Mariam

I sleep on the overnight flight from Addis, but I'm tired and weirded-out by London. It's strange to be back at the Whitt. Nothing much has changed, except that they have a Costa Coffee in the café zone serving chocolate donuts. I'll have to watch out for those or I'll be waddling around the corridors. It's a shock to see how fat British people are getting, and I will never get over the sight of the yellow-grey cancer patients in their backless gowns smoking fags outside the big glass doors of the entrance hall.

The interview goes well. It's just a formality really. All of us on the panel agree on the front runner. She's very able. I think I can get on with her. It's a dream job for me, with a dream team. Exactly what I'd been hoping for and a fantastic role to go back to. Inexplicably, I feel a bleak pinch of dissatisfaction; I decide to put it down to being under-slept.

I meet with my old mate Karen for a drink in Paddington station. She's in her work gear, though since she's based in Shoreditch, her work gear is funkier than anything I'd wear out clubbing. It's a long time since I thought about fashion. I'm two years behind every trend. She'll sort me out pretty quickly though. Bring me back up to speed. She's looking forward to having me back. She's getting a couple of grey hairs in that dark bob of hers, and she's compensated for the dark circles under her eyes with kohl eyeliner. Her boyfriend

Gary was a two-timing dickhead so she's ditched him, but time is running out for her to have kids. She's seeing a new bloke she met through Guardian Soulmates. He seems nice, but it's hard to tell. She's looked into freezing her eggs. I want to tell her about John, but it strikes me there is really nothing much to tell. The memory of that briefest brush of his lips against mine. She'd think it hilarious that I went all the way to Ethiopia and met a British man. And a doctor. I always said I'd never date a doctor. Ah well, you live and learn.

We drink wine and eat nuts and gabble our news at each other. It's lovely to see her, but small flashes of fear keep undercutting the relief of familiarity. In a few months, I'll be back. This will be it. And London life's so busy, and the transport's so tedious, that I probably won't see Karen much more than I have while I've been living in Africa. The ease of everything is seductive, soporific even, but I can already feel a twitchy disappointment that will soon overwhelm me if I don't find an outlet for it. I'll have to track down the Ethiopian and Eritrean communities that live in Tufnell Park; perhaps I'll get a teacher and improve my Amharic. So that I can be more useful when I go back to visit. The thought of visiting Ethiopia makes me so excited that a lump comes to my throat. I think of the setting sun behind the purple jacarandas on Roosevelt and I already feel nostalgic.

Karen hugs me off onto the Gloucester train and I settle down for the journey. It's only been a year, but the white chalk hills seem fascinating, like a foreign landscape. My book lies open in my lap, unread. I can't take my eyes off them. There are so many ways to live.

Mum meets me at the station and we hug on the platform. Outside London, it still attracts some attention, a black woman, a white parent.

"Look at you! You're such a skinny minny! Oh, it's good to see you," Mum says into my hair.

When we finally pull apart and we've fought over my case, which I insist on carrying because of her bad back, she has to have a hand on me, on my sleeve, on my hair, like she's not quite sure I'm real. She seems smaller than I remembered, but she seems well.

I unpack in my old room. It was redecorated years ago, but the view's the same; a long golden valley, hill tops with crests of trees. It's stored in my head like a photo in an album, unchanging. Tomorrow I'll walk out into it, noting the changes, in it and me, but today I'm still arriving. The transition is impossible. I can't exist in two places at once, and right now my head's still in Ethiopia.

I unpack the presents I've been hoarding for them; bags of green Harar coffee for Jim, Mum's 'friend', to roast in the little pan I've brought him, scarves for Mum, and necklaces made of coloured paper beads, painted wooden birds, a ridiculous T-shirt with the face of Emperor Tewodros on that I couldn't resist. Jim can wear it for gardening.

After, Mum and I sit at the table with mugs of camomile tea. Physically, she's let go of me, but her eyes don't leave me. She's looking for clues, stories I haven't told her.

"You're thin," she says.

"Slim. I'm healthy. Haven't been sick since the first year. I think I've got the better of those Ethiopian bugs."

"We were only in Ethiopia for a week when we came to collect you. I think I was on the toilet for most of that time," she remembers. "So tell me. How is it?"

"Hard," I say. "Good. Sad. Wonderful." I start to laugh. "I can't believe I'm coming home in a few months."

"Are you? Really? Coming home?" she asks. I'm surprised she needs to ask, but it's a genuine question.

"Of course. My time is up. I'll go back to the Whitt."

"Are you ready to come back?" Her hand slips over mine, long white fingers twining through my dark ones.

"It's what I planned," I say, feeling defensive.

"I know. But... listen, love. If you want to stay longer, it's fine. You shouldn't come back for me. There's things there that are holding you, I can see. Perhaps you should hold off a bit."

"Look, I'm ready to leave," I lie. "I can't drag it out forever. What would I stay for?"

She looks at me strangely, like she's been talking to an idiot.

"Hang on a minute," she says. She goes into the other room and comes back with an envelope. She takes it out, unfolds it, and slides it over to me. Her hands are shaking. The piece of paper is in Amharic, it has a stamp, and some official-looking titles. The only words I can easily read are typed, Paul and June Foster.

"What is this?" I ask. I'm pretty sure I know what it is. What I mean is, why is she giving this to me now?

"It's your adoption certificate. Mariam, I think you should have it."

I can't breathe.

"You know I don't want to think about all that," I mutter.

"I know you don't. You never have done. You used to shout and put your hands over your ears when you were a child. But that was years ago, Mariam. You're a grown-up now and I think you need to see this." She sounds impatient.

"Why?" I pout. I don't want this. I would like to put my hands over my ears and shout, but it's not allowed. Why is she doing this now?

"Because, because, there's a name on it. Somewhere on here. I can't read it but... Your birth mother's name. I don't want you to miss your chance. I know you don't need my permission, but for what it's worth, you have it."

The paper swims in front of my eyes. I feel as panicky as if this birth mother was going to walk into the room. My Amharic reading is slow to say the least, but suddenly I can't read the *fidel* characters at all. I don't want to know anything about her. I stare at the paper dumbly.

"You think I should try to find her," I say flatly.

"Well, that's up to you, of course," Mum says quietly. "I thought, I always thought, that you might come to ask me for this one day. I expected it. Especially when you went to Ethiopia. And though that idea is hard, I thought it was inevitable, that you might want to find her. If you really don't, that's your decision. But I can't help thinking that you've never really let yourself think about it properly. And this might be your last chance. She'll be old, for an Ethiopian, if she's still alive."

"She's probably not alive. She probably died years and years ago."

"Perhaps. But alive or dead, perhaps you could find out something about her. It doesn't change anything between us, Mariam. I love you. As far as I'm concerned, you're my daughter and always will be."

"Then I don't need to know her," I mutter. At the same time, Mum's permission is flaring inside me, triggering chains of possibilities. I'd imagined those possibilities so many times. I'd imagined them, then flattened them and then put them away in a box, never to be spoken of. But now, something has changed. I feel braver. I've always known

I had Mum's unspoken permission, it's just that this is the first time I have allowed myself to hear it. It is the baby that has changed me. I am more honest, more courageous than before.

"I might hate her."

"You might. She might be really annoying, like your Aunty Linda," she smiles, trying to make light of it.

"So what's the point?"

"Because you'll always wonder, won't you? And because if she's alive she will remember you, as you were. As a baby. That's important."

"She probably had lots of children afterwards. She won't have memories of me. And anyway, I'm not that person anymore."

"She gave birth to you. She will remember."

My eyes are coming into focus. I scan down the page. I see the title 'Mother's name' and know I have to read on and if I read on I will have to start looking for her.

Wodare Haile Mikael, it says. My birth mother's name. I read it aloud to my other mother, my adoptive mother, my real mother. Mum. My birth mother's age is written next to her name: sixteen. Same age as T'irunesh. I do the maths. If she's alive, she will be fifty-one years old.

"That sounds right. You were nearly three when we took you. You'd been in the orphanage for two years. She had you until you were a year old. That was unusual. Usually babies come at birth. You had some time with her. I leave it in your hands, love. I just wanted you to have the choice."

I look at her, anxious brown eyes, greying hair. I know every bit of her body, the feel of her skin, the smell of her, with the intimacy of her own child. I lean in and wrap my arms around her.

She breathes into my hair. I feel her breath warm against my scalp.

"We looked after each other, didn't we, by not talking about the hard stuff? I think perhaps we should have done though. I think it needs facing. Even if it means falling apart a bit. If you need to fall apart, I'll be here to help you pick up the bits, Mariam. You're my daughter."

"Love you, Mum," I sniff.

"You too," she says back.

That night I lie in bed looking at the stars over the valley. The same sky blankets Ethiopia. I think about the woman called Wodare who carried me in her body and fed me with her milk then gave me away. I think about love and what it means. I think about the baby and hope she's safe. Lastly, I think about John and wonder what he does with his evenings. I think about going back, to him, to them perhaps. In the darkness, I smile.

The next day, me, Mum and Jim go into town, to potter around the pre-Christmas shops. I pick up some new clothes in one of the shops on the high street. I get a cardigan for Seble, a pretty blouse for Rahel. For Betty, I get a notebook, and for John... nothing. I don't know what he'd want. And there is nothing that would not seem too trivial for the things that are passing between us.

Mum and Jim head to the fruit shop and I dive into a supermarket to stock up on the things I can't get in Addis: tins of salmon, chocolate, biscuits, nuts. The choice is overwhelming; there are dozens of brands of biscuits. Free-from, organic, special offer, two for one. The choice is deadening, disgusting, fascinating. I can't avoid reading all the information on the packaging. Because I can; because it's not in Arabic, or Greek or any of the other languages that imported food comes labelled with. I've been craving this stuff for months, but now that I'm here I don't want it any more. It's taking too long. I grab a few packets and move on.

I find myself in the brightly lit baby aisle and I pause. Do I dare buy her something? It feels like a dangerous decision. In Ethiopia, you don't buy baby clothes or a bed before the baby comes. You shouldn't tempt fate. She's thirty-eight weeks. Still small, though she's basically reached term. Hanging on a small rack are some babygrows. I reach out to finger the plush fabric. One is yellow like duckling fluff. I place it in my shopping basket and feel stupidly excited.

At the checkout, the shop assistant comments on it.

"Oh, cute! Makes me wish mine were babies still," she says wistfully. "They grow up so fast."

I smile awkwardly, hoping she doesn't ask who it's for. But she just rings up the bill.

Afterwards, standing outside the shop waiting for Mum and Jim, my phone buzzes in my pocket. The number is prefaced +251... Ethiopia. My heart jumps in my chest.

Then a man's voice.

"Mariam, it's John. Can you hear me? The line's bad. I'm sorry to ring like this but it's the baby. We're losing her..."

The baby

She has been lost in the fever for days. It consumes her. She lives in the moment. And each moment is bad. She cannot remember a time before it, nor imagine a time when it will pass. She does not want to live but she has no choice. She is stronger than they predicted.

The infection has many textures. Sometimes it is like a hairy blanket that not only suffocates her from above, but also pushes filaments into her lungs, filling them with fur. At other times, it is like a silken vein of ice that slips through the chambers of her heart. But she has no experience of fur or ice. She cannot contain her feelings in thought; she must feel them in all their untrammelled foulness. She does not cry. She cannot shiver, so she pants. Her skin prickles with heat, then waves of chills sweep over her. Her organs are swollen, and lying in the bed makes her back ache to numbness. No one comes to lift her, to give her respite from the supine position.

Finally, she is lifted and held. She is rocked, a firm hand behind her head, a warm body next to her chest. As she is brought upright she feels her organs slip against each other, tumble through the cavities of her abdomen. She is too weak to protest, but she squeezes her brow into a furrowed frown. The frown stays. Her face is pinched tight, anxious. Even the goodness of the warmth, the arms cannot take away the disquiet. She must battle on. She is exhausted by it. She lets the body that holds her take a little of the strain and it helps. After a while she drifts into fitful sleep filled with voices.

First a man.

"I gave strict instructions that she not be removed from the incubator."

Then a woman.

"Let's speak plainly, Dr Tadesse. I don't give a shit about your instructions. I know this baby better than anyone else and I know that she needs to be held. She's sick. She could be dying. You should have told me!"

"I didn't make her sick. I've been trying to keep her alive. You were taking an interview. It was deemed best not to disturb you."

"That's rubbish. You knew I would come back and complicate things. Draw things out. You wanted her to slip away so you could say my little project was a failure and go back to normal."

"Mariam, I will pretend you didn't say that. You should remember who you are talking to. You insult me. If you're suggesting I wanted her dead...! I took the Hippocratic oath."

"But she's in your way. You said yourself you've no room for her. It would be so much easier—"

"Perhaps it would be. You are too attached to this child. You've let your personal feelings influence your professional behaviour for too long. You must let her leave the hospital. If this child recovers, as soon as she recovers, I am sending her to the orphanage. My decision is final."

"Go to hell."

The sound of a door swishing shut. The baby's eyelids flutter. She can feel the chemicals boiling from the woman's skin and they join the fire and poison of her infection. The woman's sweat is bitter, laced with adrenalin, cortisol, things she cannot name, but she can smell and taste. They fill her with disgust and the urge to escape, but she hasn't the energy to protest. More talking. Then a new voice, a male one, this one urgent, serious.

"I saw Tadesse in the corridor. What on earth did you say to him?"

"I told him some home truths."

"That was unwise."

"I don't care about wise any more, John. Wise leaves her lying alone in an incubator for five days nearly dead with an infection. You said you'd look after her."

"And I have been. I've done what I could do without going against hospital rules."

The woman's reply blurts up from her belly but anger traps in her throat.

"Since when did you care about rules? We both know you're quite capable of making the rules up as you go along."

The man has moved away from the woman. He speaks in a level voice.

"What does that mean?"

"You know exactly what that means. For once in your life could you not speak out for what you believe in? This hospital has made you cowardly. It has you on a leash. Where's the man who saved Lidet? I thought you knew how important this is to me."

"I do know how important this is to you, but I'm thinking about the long term. This baby's care at this hospital depends on playing by the rules. So does my job. And yours."

"Don't you dare patronise me, John. You know what you are? You're compromised. Stop being professional and start being human! This baby may not have a long term. I trusted you to care for her."

The baby stiffens as waves of shaking take over the body she lies on. She writhes briefly, a protest against this emotion, these hissing, strangled voices, but the effort exhausts her and she slumps. She feels a hot drop of liquid fall onto the top of her head. Then another.

"Put the baby down a moment, Mariam. You're not helping her, the state you're in."

The baby feels the woman's diaphragm spasm as she struggles to control her voice.

"I thought she was dead. When I saw her. In the incubator. I thought she was dead... and part of me, I can't say it. Part of me knew it would be simpler that way, for me, I mean. I know what Dr Tadesse means. I shouldn't be feeling like this. I had to come, as soon as I heard. I haven't slept for thinking about her. John, I don't know what to do."

"You're exhausted. You've travelled 8,000 miles in three days. I'll stay with her. I won't hold her but I'll keep my hand on her so she knows I'm there. You should get some sleep. She's stable. You'll be more use to her when you've slept. We'll talk about this later."

The baby is passed from one body to another. She feels the cool cloth of the man's jacket and opens her eyes to squint at the whiteness of it before she is slid back into the incubator to fight the legions of germs that want her dead.

Tewodros

Tewodros is lost in the old stories, the ones his father used to tell him. He has a sudden memory of his father's feet; slim feet with long toes and cracked yellow heels. He always used to sit at his father's feet when he told his stories.

The prince of the hyenas has died. All the animals must come to the funeral to pay tribute. The donkeys are afraid. They know that if they go into the hyenas' lair they will be eaten. But they know that they will be eaten if they do not attend to show respect. Frightened, they begin to sing.

Oh, fearsome beasts who hunt by dark,
The moonlight echoes with your barks.
Your teeth so sharp, your eyes so bright,
Your meat is black but your shit is white.
There is no heir to fill the throne,
Your son is gone! Our lord is gone!

They pretend to weep, willing the tears to flow so that the hyenas will not see their pretence and eat them. It seems that they have fooled them, but as the donkeys shuffle away the dead hyena's uncle calls out, "What have you brought us mourners to eat?"

The donkeys panic. The hyenas surround them, edging closer, teeth dripping with drool.

"We have nothing to give you, sir," one brays.

The hyenas snicker and growl their disapproval.

"Give us your lips," the uncle demands.

What choice do they have? To pacify the throng of hyenas, the donkeys form a line and one by one each submits to a razor swipe of claw that slices off their soft brown lips. The hyenas scuffle and snarl and snap for the fleshy titbits. The donkeys, dripping blood, try to edge away. They cannot cover their teeth with their lips, nor use their hooves to cover their exposed teeth.

"You!" screams the uncle hyena, pointing to a long-toothed donkey. "I can see your yellow teeth! Could it be... could it be that you are grinning at me? Yes, I think you are mocking our grief!"

Too late the donkeys see they have been tricked. They were never going to get out of this alive. The hyenas descend on them in a stinking, snarling scrum, tearing them to pieces.

Before the last donkey dies, he looks up at the hyenas and says:

Wicked beasts, we came in faith,
With comfort. That was our mistake.
For selfish reasons, don't contrive
Excuses just to take our lives.

The Eritreans had crossed the border at Badme and many Ethiopian troops were killed, then and in the retaliation that followed. For a month afterwards the house was full of visitors, sitting with his mother, holding her hand, praying with her. The priest came often. Tewodros was afraid of him. The priest looked at him askance, as if the devil was in the same room. Snatches of the Bible took him to the high dusty lands where his father was.

Yet have I set my kingdom on the holy hill of Zion. You have put gladness in my heart. You are my defence. The Lord is my strength and shield. You are as a lamp to my feet and a light to my path.

The holy hill of Zion got mixed up in his head with the great fortress Meqdella, which got mixed up with the holy rock church of Debre Damo.

So when the unit Tewodros's father was in was moved from Adigrat to Mekelle his mother had rejoiced. Mekelle was further south, further away from the border where the troubles were. The people were one people with the Eritreans, brothers and sisters. They shared a language, they were cousins. Now his father would just have to wait out the war. Army life is mostly about waiting, and being the son of a farmer he'd grazed enough cattle to be good at waiting.

No one expected the bombing. And no one knew what Tewodros's father was doing near the school at Ayder. It was his day off. Perhaps he was on an errand. Perhaps he had climbed to look at the view. Perhaps, and this is what Tewodros told himself in the years to come, he was missing his sons and had wanted to be near children. To remember what innocence looked like.

The plane, an Eritrean Mig, flew over the school and dropped its bomb. When they heard the screaming and saw the smoke and fire, townspeople came running, parents came running. Tewodros's father came running. The pilot flew down the valley, turned the plane around and flew back to drop another load. The shrapnel ripped out Tewodros's father's stomach.

The army sent a messenger to deliver the news the day they saw the footage of the attack on the television. The screams that came from his mother made him block his ears with his hands and rock. He wanted to escape to his mountaintop, but when he needed a fit a fit would not come. How was he to believe that his father was dead? His absence was no different from the long periods when he was away on manoeuvres. He could not make himself understand it. The tears would not fall. His mother chastised him with red eyes, but he could not cry. The house filled up with women, weeping and keening, shaking their heads wildly as if they could shake off the heavy cloak of grief that clung to them. He knew if the Eritrean bomber walked into the room that they would rip him limb from limb and smear their faces with his blood. The old justice.

The priest came. He spoke in a low monotonous whisper to his mother, who quietened and snivelled. *A man's heart plans his way, but the Lord directs his steps.* The priest told her to accept the mysterious decisions of the Lord and asked her to see it as a sign. *Do not boast about tomorrow for you do not know what a day may bring forth.* He asked her to look to herself, to her family and see if they could not find reason for this punishment. They should pray to God for forgiveness and mend their ways to ensure the ascent of his father's soul to heaven. *The Lord has made all for himself, yes, even the wicked for the day of doom.* It was only a split second, but he caught his mother's eye as she glanced in his direction. Then she bit her lip and bowed her head. He saw then how it would be. He was a donkey. Damned, whatever he did. The priest would blame him and his mother would harden against him.

For selfish reasons, don't contrive
Excuses just to take our lives.

The priest had never liked him. For the first time since the news he raised up his head and glowered at the man, who, walnut-faced and self-satisfied, continued with his drone.

For they eat the bread of wickedness and drink the wine of violence.

Tewodros could feel the anger rising in him. His namesake, the emperor, was stirring in defiance. Well then, since he could not suffer the insult in silence, he would drink the wine of violence. He would be a scourge.

Had not the priests who counselled the emperor tried to weaken him with mollifying, blaming advice? How long had he gone along with it before he had seen the poison that they planted, seen how self-serving they were? Of course, it suited them to make the population passive, dependent. Donkeys to hyenas. Lambs to the slaughter. It was the priests who lined their pockets with gold and their soft beds with fleece. Their guest intoned on. The guttural Ge'ez sounded like blasphemy on his lips. His father's death deserved more than to be suffered or borne. It needed action, anger. He stood and clenched his fists. The priest glared at him and gestured to him to sit with such a look of contempt that something broke in the boy and seeing the priest's long staff lying on the earth floor next to him, he lunged for it. His mother screamed and clawed and the priest cowered as the boy's blows rained down on his shoulders. The silver cross on the tip of the staff caught the light; it gleamed and glowed, confirming to him with every strike that the true cause of righteous indignation was his. He rounded on the man, herding him from the house. Standing panting on the bare earth he threw the staff to one side. The mountains grew closer and Meqdella rose up before him, filling his lungs with the ether of his great deed. The Lord, the true one, had blessed him and he knew he had done right. *Open my eyes, that I may see marvellous things.*

Mariam

We are walking in the Entoto hills that rise above Addis Ababa. Our route takes us near the rock church. Washa Mikael, it's called. This saint, Teklehaimanot, is meant to have lived there. All I know about him is that he's famous for standing on one leg to honour God. I suppose there are all sorts of ways to show your devotion, if that's what turns you on. Anyway, he stood on one leg for so long that the other leg fell off. The locals preserved it. If you're really faithful, once a year they bring the mummified leg out to wash it and you can drink the washing water. As if there weren't enough ways to get sick in Ethiopia. Still, I suppose if you believe it probably makes you feel better. My housekeeper Seble will be first in line. Sometimes I wish I shared that comfort.

Betty is striding out ahead of me, black skin shining in the sunlight, the silver beads in her hair glinting. The hillside rolls down towards Kotebe, the new town with its new Chinese road, the town that will one day eat up the land we stand on. But for now, clusters of wood and mud houses shelter the farmers who live off the land. Their women rake the leaves from the forest to make smoky fires. The penalty for cutting a tree is years in prison. The grass is so clean, raked free of leaf litter and undergrowth, that it feels like we are in a well-manicured park. The eucalyptus trees sway against a blue sky, and small clusters of sheep and goats nibble the yellowed grass. A donkey, front hoof tethered to its opposite back hoof, moves slowly in a ditch, munching at some thistly plant. Further on, towards the church compound itself, a group of runners in Ethiopian colours, red, yellow and green, are warming up. The famous marathon runner Haile Gebre Selassie has a training school up here for elite athletes.

The air is fresh above the city. You could be in the countryside instead of vertical minutes from the town, which stretches out, grey and glittering below our plateau, below the encircling peaks of Yerer, Wuchacha and Zuqualla. The airport to the left makes a bald place among the building works. To the west is the hospital. She's there. Dressed in a yellow duckling fluff babygrow.

"I don't have to ask you who you're thinking about," says Betty, doubling back, placing a soft hand on my arm. "Come, let's find a spot and talk."

We sit down under a tall bare-barked eucalyptus, laying a blanket down against the biting ants. She's brought coffee and I have brought Seble's excellent cinnamon buns. We are friends again after our fight. It took a few weeks for me to face her, but I am glad. I need my friend to talk sense to me, especially now. I'm scared of the feelings I have. They are bigger than me. Important. Impatient. She is looking at me with those dark wise eyes, brooding over her steaming coffee like some sort of oracle.

"I thought I could do it," I say quietly. "I thought I could save her life, then let her go. But I'm not strong enough." Dr Tadesse was right. The personal and professional are a dangerous mix.

"I'm glad to hear it," sniffs Betty.

"What do you mean?"

"Your idea of strong, Mariam, is building walls to keep the pain out. Let the pain in. Let your love out." She reaches over to stroke my arm.

My pride is shattered. I am a cripple. Without my emotional crutches, I am writhing on the ground, no use to anyone.

"You make it sound so easy."

"No. To be vulnerable is the hardest thing in the world. You will want to die. But then, you will be more alive. I believe this."

I shake my head.

"How did you get so wise? Oh, Betty. This isn't fair. I am a midwife. We're meant to be practical, efficient. I can't do this. I need to know what to *do*."

"Feel first, do later," she says archly, Yoda-like, licking the cinnamon sugar from her long fingers.

I can't make sense of her words.

"But I think there's something wrong with my feelings. They tell me these crazy things," I mutter.

She lets out a cackle that sends the donkey startling back in its ditch, and reaches over to hug me, nearly knocking me over.

"I love you, *Mariame*. You're so funny. Always looking for order and control. Life is messy. Love is messier still. You think it's simple? Hey, I didn't tell you. Solomon had an affair when he was working in Mekele."

"No... Oh, Betty, I'm so sorry." I am appalled but she brushes my apology away.

"Yeah. He couldn't keep his dick in his pants. But," she giggles guiltily, "I did a bad thing. When I found out I was so angry, I got very drunk and I slept with one of his best friends." She tips her head to one side, shrugging her shoulders.

"No!"

"But it's OK. We've talked about it. I've forgiven him. And he has forgiven me. He has almost forgiven his friend. I love my husband and he loves me. He's not going to work away so much. Love. It's messy, you see?"

"I don't know if I would forgive him so easily," I say defensively.

"Yeah, well. Nobody's perfect. Not even me," she laughs. "Oh, that one-night stand, it was so awful. The sex was just the worst. It was a terrible mistake. Really, we're stronger now. You have to trust. To hope for better. Shit happens, as they say."

"Hmmm..." She looks OK. She looks better than OK. She positively glows. Tranquil.

"So. Come on. The baby. How is she?" Betty asks and I feel excited to speak of her. I have been longing to talk about her. She sucks my thoughts towards her like an irresistible magnet, my brain throbs with thinking of her.

"She's better. I mean, the infection is cured. She's weakened, but growing. It's like she's moved into a new phase; almost like the infection was a kind of birth, a fight. She's nearly term. She's done the extra gestation she needed. I mean, she still needs time to recover, but for the first time, I'm really hopeful."

"That's wonderful."

"It's like she's decided she's going to live. I really think she will live. If only they'll let her stay, if only the bloody pig-headed administration will give her just another few weeks."

I sigh.

"Betty, I said some things to John I shouldn't have. Mean things. I was tired. Upset. It's hard for him, navigating the hospital politics. I haven't made it any easier for him."

"Oh, he's a big boy and he's been here for years. He's had a lot of practice. He'll survive. I'm glad the baby's stronger. I have more milk for her. Stop by and collect it on the way home."

"You should see the folds of fat on her legs. She's so

chubby. And lots of dark curly hair. She can almost hold her head up by herself, though she still bobbles it about like a little pigeon. The nurses take her on little walks around the ward, to stimulate her. They call her the little queen."

"Does she smile yet?"

"Not yet. Most of the time she looks so serious, like she's figuring out a problem, little pouting mouth. She's one of those babies that really looks like she's lived before.

"An old soul."

"Yes. But *so* strong," I gush proudly. "I'm not used to seeing this character, to seeing her express herself. She used to be so silent. The whole time, since she was born. Hardly a sound. But yesterday, when I left her, when I put her down, she cried. Proper crying. It was awful. I mean, it went right through me. I could hardly think straight. Her face; she just looked so lost. So pitiful."

"But you had to leave?"

"I had an appointment, yes. But I cancelled it. Because every time I tried to leave, she'd cry. The whole ward was watching, wondering what I was going to do. I'd rock her to sleep then try to slide her back into her cot, and she'd wake with this start and wail. Like she knew it might be the last time. In the end, she slept, and I crept away. I felt so awful knowing she'd wake to find me gone."

I didn't tell her what I'd felt, more keenly than before. That as much as the baby, it was Ethiopia that I was trying to leave. Trying to extricate myself from its painful, wonderful, addictive grip.

"They're going to take her soon then?"

"Yes. The police will come to escort her to the orphanage. Like a little illegitimate criminal." Before I can think better of it, I blurt, "Betty, won't you adopt her?"

"What?"

"She could stay with you. I would support her, financially. I would visit. She could grow up with your children."

"Mariam, no. Don't even think it. I have never met this child."

"She's lovely. Really beautiful. I think she's escaped side effects. Of course, we can't be sure yet, but I really think she's going to be normal, no problems. She's easy."

Betty leans back from me shaking her head.

"It's never crossed your mind, has it?"

"What?"

It is sinking in that she has said no and she means it. It was the only solution I could think of. I had hoped to persuade her. A great wash of bleak water sluices through my chest.

"What hasn't crossed my mind?"

"That you could adopt her yourself."

The words seem to have an echo. A time delay. They buzz through the still mountain air. I hear the sound of them, but the meaning, the import takes longer to reach me. I look at my hands in my lap. Of course I have thought it. I have been hoping for, dreading this moment. But her saying it makes it real. I have to confront my fears.

"They won't let me. I'm not married. What about my job in the UK? What about going home?"

"Those are obstacles. Put off the job. Stay. Nothing's impossible. You love her, don't you?"

I nod. The realisation of it hits me so hard that the sobs come before I can push them down. I feel the hard place in the centre of me soften and unclench.

"It hurts. It hurts." I gulp. Betty holds me and we rock beneath the eucalyptus. A little way off, the donkey stops chewing mid-mouthful to look as us intently, a long strand of thistle hanging from its whiskery lips.

Tewodros

He knows, of course, which one it will be. It will be the one who touched him. Last week, she handed him some purple trousers from the hospital. He held them to his nose and inhaled. She did not want to talk that time, did not want to write for him, as she'd done before, but moved on quickly without speaking. He wondered at that. She'd been so friendly before. But then he remembered that the last time they'd spoken the police had come and perhaps she was afraid they would come again. Perhaps she was protecting him. Of course, he could defend himself, but that day, she'd stood between him and the policeman. He knew, then, that she was the one he would have to take. Her hand was shaking when she handed him back his paper. She was afraid. Well, then, he must teach her to be strong.

It's cowardly to pick an acquaintance, especially after all the help she gave him. He should really go for a stranger, someone to whom he has no obligations. And then there is the fact that she is not truly *ferenji*, not like the hostages the emperor took. She's British, but she looks Ethiopian. Of course, if she had white skin and yellow hair it would be harder for him to lay hands on her when he takes her. He would not be able to look at her. But will she give him as much bargaining power? It is a shame she is not American. Everyone knows that Americans are worth more than other people. However, he has seen the great gate of the *Engliz* Embassy with its lion and unicorn. And it can be no coincidence that George is the patron saint of the English.

The English will come for her. In the end, they honour their word. All the way from England, they came, to liberate the emperor's hostages. All the way, with mules and telegraphs and railways. With breech-loading Sniders and Gurkha cavalry. All the way to his mountain fortress, to Meqdella itself. When they come for her, he will share his list with them. He will ask for no reward. To see his country great again will be enough.

He feels uncomfortable about all this, but in time she will understand. She seems like an understanding person. He sees her every morning coming to the hospital. She looks thinner, nervous. Perhaps she has troubles with her work. She will be able to tell him when he has her to himself.

Sometimes he follows her part of her way home. She doesn't know he does this. He spots her, marching up the hill and hurriedly he picks up his sack and tracks her route. He cannot keep up with her pace, not in his broken sandals, but she is easy to follow. She stands out in the crowd with her purposeful style of walking. Some days she keeps to the main roads, but recently she has started to take the cut-through that passes his secret room. This in itself shows him the suitability of his choice of hostage. Or should he say the emperor's choice, for it is the emperor that directs him now, through the touchstone of the list.

He has begun amassing supplies for her. There is no bed, of course, only cardboard, but she will understand. He has a blanket to cover her. She will perhaps be afraid and think he wants to lie with her, but he will tell her that his mind is on other things. It would of course be nice to lie next to her soft body, to smell her clean smell, but he does not want to make her feel afraid.

There are several bottles of Coke for her, bought with coins that passers-by have thrust at him. Two packets of biscuits. A bag of rolls. He will bring bananas. His own body has become weak on his diet of bread and Coca-Cola. He should eat meat. He needs his strength. Who knows how long he will have to keep her before those with power and wisdom will listen?

Last week it struck him that there would be nowhere for her to relieve herself. The thought had made him blush. Though he himself thinks nothing of emptying his bowels in public, she is not like him. She is used to her privacy. It was a problem. He partially solved it by finding a plastic bucket in the rubble. He will turn away when she needs to perform and then, every day, he will dispose of her waste to keep the little room smelling sweet. If it were Meskel, he could fill the room with yellow blossoms from the wasteland to show her she is welcome, but it is not, and anyway, no flowers grow amid the rubble, only thistles.

He is not a man for speaking, but they will talk. He will tell her about the emperor, and the list. About George and the lessons that Ethiopia must learn in order to become great.

There is a story about a man thrown into a pit that serves as a prison. There is no roof to contain the prisoner, but the jailer explains, "This is Ethiopia. If a prisoner tries to climb out, his countrymen will soon pull him back into prison." His brethren squabble among themselves, Amhars with Oromos, Muslims with Christians, when they should unite in the old glory. Strong men like him must slip the grip of jealous compatriots and show just what is possible.

The emperor told him they will listen. He feels uneasy at the phrase. He does not know *exactly* who 'they' are. Perhaps Meles might have listened, but he is dead. They set up tents for people to grieve for the prime minister in. The people came and wept and wailed and ripped their clothes and Tewodros rocked in his ditch at the memory of his own father's death. He keeps his head down when he passes posters of Meles but he does not hold him accountable. When a farmer turns soldier, he makes a man's decision.

The fits are coming unasked-for now. Sometimes several a day. He may have to tie her up, so that she does not think to escape during one of them. He needs his fits, to give him direction, inspiration, but they leave him weakened and sapped of strength. Sometimes he loses the sight in one eye and a black pressing weight seems to come over one side of his face. He rests then, and soon it passes, but the tingling stays down the left side of his body and sometimes his lower lip hangs for an hour, leaking drool. It is his burden and his joy.

When he stands in the bright light and white breeze of Meqdella, he knows the price is worth paying. Recently the peaks have been higher than he could imagine; cold clean air, so thin it scorches his lungs; light so pure that it makes him laugh for joy, empty-headed with alpine asphyxia. And then the lumpen return to his failing body; the stench, the pain, the inadequacy. He returns with secrets, gifts for the good of all, but he does not know how long he will be able to keep on journeying to that bright land of inspiration. Time is running out.

He will have to take her soon.

Mariam

After our walk on Entoto, Betty tells me to go home. To sleep on it. But I can't wait. I need to act. So I seek out John. I feel guilty for how harshly I spoke to him but I am beyond shame. I need his help. As I dial his number I remember the words I used: 'compromised, cowardly'. I have no right to ask him for anything.

He picks up on the third ring. His voice is muffled; he has a cold. Brought on by spending so much overtime with the baby, I think guiltily. He is at home, resting. His tone is cool, and his distance hurts, however much I had been expecting it. He expresses no surprise when I tell him I need to see him. I am to come to him. I think he has finally decided against any further involvement. Too emotional, and about to leave. He will have labelled me 'unstable'. More trouble than I am worth. But he agrees to meet me at least.

I hand my phone to the taxi driver and John speaks to him in Amharic, directing the dilapidated blue Toyota up into the hills above the Italian embassy. I am thrown around in the back; I don't care. It matches how I'm feeling. I need the distraction of movement. Stillness suffocates me. Up here, ancient cedar trees encroach on the road; between the wattle-and-daub huts with their yellow-and-blue plastic tarps, between the tin Arkebe shops selling their garish Fanta and tins of Nido baby milk, there are old compounds.

John is waiting outside one of them, hands in his pockets,

looking at his feet. Same frayed blue shirt, but this time he is wearing jeans and trainers. He looks younger. Scruffy. He's got a couple of days' stubble, though the hair is so white-blond it's barely noticeable. He keeps his head down as I pay the taxi driver, then ushers me into his house.

His compound is shady, a cobbled courtyard with big unkempt plants in pots. The house is stone, with a long porch, and I step onto polished wooden floors. Inside, the fluorescent light is dim and the curtains are half drawn. There's a map of Ethiopia on one wall, some Kenyan-looking throws. It doesn't give much away. It feels like a house that doesn't get lived in much. It's chilly too. He should be keeping warm. There's an unlit fire in the hearth.

He gestures me towards a sofa, miming a sore throat as an excuse for his silence, then disappears into the kitchen.

I have to clear a pile of paper away to make a place to sit. Financial documents. Bank books. What's making John take stock? None of my business. I sit with my head in my hands, my right foot twitching and tapping with anxiety until he returns.

He's holding two cups of hot tea. He places one on the small table in front of me and then retreats to the back wall, as far away from me as it is possible to be, where he leans, sipping from his own. I can't tell if he's keeping his germs away from me, or if he's putting as much space between us as possible. Possibly he finds me repugnant. I don't know anything anymore. I am pleased to discover he's sugared the tea heavily; I need sweetness, warmth, comfort. Two of the three he has given me.

"So," he says, his voice breaking on the word. He is ill. He fixes me with blank blue eyes that have dark circles beneath them.

"I had no right to speak to you that way. Please forgive me. It's not true. I'm so sorry," I whisper, putting the tea down and spilling most of it in the saucer.

"Of course," he nods coolly.

I have hurt him. He is so far away. I have to hold on to the sofa. I hope I have not lost him completely.

"John, please. I need. I need to tell you something. I'm not going to leave." The words catch him with the cup halfway to his lips.

He thinks better of sipping, and puts the cup down and pushes it away from him with one finger as if protecting it from the scene that may follow.

"You're staying now?" he says flatly, but I think I catch the slightest trace of sarcasm. He has every right to be angry with me. "What happened?" His voice is disinterested, but he moves closer, pulling himself out a dining room chair and sitting on it. The effort makes him cough; he places a hand flat over his ribs and turns his face away from me.

I give him time to recover.

"I can't leave. Not now."

For a brief moment, his face opens, then he realises it is not him I am staying for.

"The baby?" he confirms, looking at his shoes.

I am not playing this well. My chest hurts.

"Well, tell me then," he says.

"I need to... I want to try to adopt her, John. I'm going to turn down the job in England. I'm going to adopt her!"

The admission is still such a shock that the hope blasts a smile onto my face and despite himself, I see John smiles back. The words are a tiny ray of sunlight, a shred of meaning. I want to sing them, to go to the window and shout them to anyone who will listen. In the words, I see myself carrying her over a threshold in my arms. Looking into her eyes. Holding her to me and knowing that I do not have to let her go.

There is something in my honesty that breaks our stand-off; he puts his hands to his head, his elbows resting on his knees. He stays like that, quiet. Finally, he lifts his head and looks wryly at me with one eye, exhausted by the chaos I have brought to his life. He coughs, feebly, mocking his pathetic state.

"So. A small good thing," he says. "It would be a small good thing." He smiles, but he sounds defeated. I recognise the feeling. The greatest thing I have to offer is so inadequate.

"I know it won't change anything. Not the big picture."

"That shouldn't stop you."

"I don't know why I didn't consider it before. It seemed, I don't know, forbidden. Now I'm scared how much I want it. Am I allowed to want it this much? It should be about her, shouldn't it? What if it's all about me?"

"I'm sure it isn't." He smiles wearily, running a hand through his hair. "And even if it was, would the motive matter? The end result is the same: a child will have a mother who loves her. You'll be a good mother."

I look at him with wide eyes. The words terrify me and excite me.

"I never thought I would have children. I've never wanted a child of my own. I'm not sure I know how to do it."

"Just make her feel loved," he croaks. "Let *her* know you're not going to leave."

His voice is thick. He should be in bed. I could lead him there and we could lie down together. I am strong enough to weather his sickness. I feel I caused this lovely man to be ill. I want to hold him like a boy until he is well again.

"Love is pretty much all that matters, when you come down to it," he continues. Blue, washed-out eyes. Laughter lines. Freckles. Sun-bleached brows. My mind is empty. There will be time, I think. Time for all this. This other kind of love. He said he would wait for me.

"Here. I want to show you something," he says. He goes to the sofa, locates the pile of papers I moved to the floor. He pulls out a bank book. "Look at this."

"What is it?"

"I hardly know how to explain it. It's... it's what I was, Mariam. What I have come from. But not what I want to be."

"I don't understand."

"I'm glad you don't. And I wouldn't expect you too. I don't know what I was thinking."

He opens the book and shows me the ledger. There are several thousand pounds in the account. He shuts the book, as if I should understand. When he sees that I don't, he drops his head. Finally, he speaks.

"It's a fund, Mariam. A fund for my children's school fees. Ever since I left university, every month, despite everything, I've been putting away a bit of money, to send them to the same bloody school that I went to." He looks at his feet. "You called me cowardly."

"I'm sorry, that was wrong. I was angry."

"No, don't apologise. You're right. It's true. I am cowardly. I don't even have children. But here I am with this bank book of money." Angrily he touches his head, signalling the insanity of it all. Then, defeated, he slowly touches his heart. "I keep people at arm's length, Mariam," he mutters. "I have done all my life."

"But I've met your Ethiopian family. I've seen how close you are to them. They clearly love you. I saw you with

Lidet's kids. You told me you'd chosen Lidet's family over your own."

"Yes. And I kidded myself that I'd drawn a line, between the way I was brought up, and the way I really wanted to be, but... but it was so ingrained, laid down in childhood. And so, in a kind of madness, a kind of autopilot, every month, I put pennies and pounds put away, repeating this *perversion* of love and what is important." He looks up, imploring.

There is a rawness, an honesty to him that is new. Then he goes on.

"Even though I knew it made no sense, Mariam, I would have sent my child away, perpetuated my misery, because I thought... because I believed it was better to be hard than to be hurt."

I am speechless. I daren't breathe. He is a new person to me. And to himself, perhaps.

"All this... you and the baby, it's made me question, well, everything really," he says, shaking his head in exhausted confusion. "I've closed the account. Of course, it would never have been enough, but even if it was, I would never... not now... I could never... I'll find a use for the money elsewhere." He looks up angrily. "What the hell was I thinking? What sort of bloody insanity is it to close the door, to send the people you love away?"

I bite my lip. I want to talk more, to listen more, but I need to speak too. I'm being selfish but I need his approval, just as it seems he's sought out mine. He is looking at his feet. I reach out and touch the back of his hand with the tips of my fingers. He seems startled.

"John. Next week I'm going to go to Sidama to find my birth mother. I've got her name."

"Good God, you don't do things by halves, do you?" He

laughs huskily, breaking the moment. "Shouldn't you deal with the baby first?"

"They're kind of connected. I was so afraid of finding my birth mother before. Afraid that she might reject me again I suppose. But if I'm to be a mother to this baby, I need to know her. To close the circle. There was never a big enough reason before. Now there is the baby. I hope I haven't left it too late. I hope she is still alive."

I thrust my hands between my knees to keep them still.

"But my VSO contract is finishing, and I've burnt my bridges at the hospital. The labour ward is closed for the next few months, and after what I said to Tadesse, I don't know how long I'll be allowed to keep going to the hospital. The doorman keeps letting me in, but it's only a matter of time before he'll be made to follow orders. The administration want rid of me, don't they?"

John raises an eyebrow that confirms my suspicion.

"John, whatever happens, I need to stay in Ethiopia. My visa runs out in two months. Will you write a reference for me so I can get another visa to stay? And my rental agreement runs out this month, so I'm going to need somewhere to live; I've got some savings but if, *big* if, she comes home with me, I won't be able to work for a while."

"Stay here," he says, without hesitation. "Stay in my house."

"Whoa!"

"Not like that," he says, looking embarrassed. "There's a spare room. I promise, you won't have to lock the door."

The idea makes me smile; it's more likely it would be me sneaking into his room in the night.

"I mean, please, stay here. I'm hardly here. I often work nights."

There is warmth in his offer. If this man were a friend, I would hug him and accept without question. But he is more than a friend.

"I wasn't looking for... I wasn't expecting this," I tell him.

"I know. But it makes sense."

A shaft of sunlight has penetrated the dim room and I find myself feeling warmer. The light picks out the warm red brown of the polished floor, a set of shelves overflowing with his books. The idea of living in his space is so intimate; it feels both exciting and dangerous. If I did move in, I would go through his books, read them all, find out who he is and what he thinks about the world.

"I'm glad you've made a decision to try to adopt the baby. But I don't have to tell you that it's no easy process."

"I know."

I am about to remind him that one of the biggest obstacles is that I am unmarried, but I stop myself just in time.

He shivers. He is sick and I am taking his time. I take one of the Kenyan throws and wrap it around him. He doesn't protest. Turning him so I am sitting behind him, I smooth the material onto his shoulders and begin massaging out the knots he earned waiting at the bedside of a sick child. He shifts, closes his eyes. He smells of cotton, tea, eucalyptus. He lets out a deep breath. Then, without opening his eyes, he reaches up and takes one of my hands and pulls it to his lips. A chaste kiss. To tide us over. Encouragement. I lean into him, wrapping my arms around him from behind, feeling his shoulders against my breasts. I breathe in the scent of him, and lay my face against him. The soft nape of his neck is freckled by the sun.

Then I leave him to recover. I have much to do, and little time.

The baby

<u>*St George's Hospital Discharge summary*</u>

Name: Baby X Merkato

Date of admission: 26/10/16 *Date of discharge:* 15/12/16

History: Female born from mother aged 18, para 1, mother had incomplete ANC. Neonate abandoned.

Clinical finding: Neonate was preterm, hypothermic, LBW on admission. Neonatal reflexes all depressed.

Diagnosis procedures and laboratory date: CBC, blood group and RH were sent to the laboratory on the day of admission.

Diagnosis (include all secondary diagnosis): DC preterm (34 weeks), LBW, Hypothermia, SGA

Completion of discharge – cured / improved / worse / no change / died: Neonate has improved well, weight gain excellent. Has reached near full-term. All neonatal reflexes are complete.

Future plan, appointment, other remarks: Discharge and transfer to Berhane orphanage. Follow-up weight gain and basic measurements, vaccination, follow-up care in high risk infant clinic (regular).

Mariam

As the hired car winds down into the Rift Valley, the landscape becomes incrementally different from Addis: marshier, moister, then the sight of marabou storks perching in the flat top branches of the acacias, their fleshy pink neck pouches swaying below dirty beaks. I speed past termite mounds. There are hippos in the lake. The people are a bit less uptight than their alpine neighbours.

I keep thinking, this is where I'm *from*, like my genes should be singing in some sort of recognition. I stay a night in a small hotel and spin round the sights inside a blue *bajaj* rickshaw. It doesn't take long. I drink a warm Mirinda orange in a bar under the canopy of a flame tree, then leave before the local men can make their moves. Next morning, I make the two-hour drive south from Hawassa to a straggling one-horse town in Sidama.

I don't remember my birthplace. The only nagging familiarity is the red earth and the *enset*, the false banana trees with their ripped-sail leaves and their fleshy trunks. Other than that, nothing. No meaningful flood of memories. The building is low breeze block, once white. The foyer has chipped shiny tiles that remind me of broken teeth. I don't see any children, but I can hear them out back, shouting and playing. I hear laughter and metal clanking from the kitchen. I smell *shiro*.

The receptionist asks me to sit. She is bemused by me. Perhaps she thinks I'm here to adopt. It's cool in the waiting room. The sudden chill makes me feel vulnerable; I fight the urge to run. They can't trap me here. They don't own me now. I am an adult. I came here by choice. Cold sweat prickles my armpits. This may be a terrible mistake. I make myself think of the baby; I am doing this for her. No. Not just for her. For the baby that was me. The thought soothes me – it lies on my chest like her warm body and I make myself breathe slowly so as not to disturb her sleep.

Woyzero Ayele, the head of the orphanage, is a stout woman in a mustard-coloured acrylic suit. She has gold teeth in her smile and firmly set ringlets. When I rang, she seemed unsurprised by my request to meet. I wonder how many ex-orphans come back to visit. I wonder when she'll try to extract a large donation from me. They don't look desperate, but I suppose this is the public-facing part of the orphanage. And it was never money or resources that were lacking here anyway. The stuff that costs nothing, that was what I missed.

I give her the adoption certificate and she looks at it critically. She pushes an enamelled nail over my birth mother's name.

"Wodare Haile Mikael," she reads, but I can see it means nothing to her. Perhaps it is even a false name.

I will never know if T'irunesh gave her true name. My heart begins to sink, or is it just the muscles of my feeling organ relaxing, knowing that they can now return to unrequited normality?

I have one photograph of myself at the time of adoption. It was taken at the orphanage; my publicity shot, if you like. It was the first photo my parents saw of me. I am about eighteen months old and I am propped up in a chair. I have almost no hair; my head has been shaved, to prevent lice I suppose. I am wearing a white dress that I know cannot have belonged to me. It is a dress to signify gender rather than a decorative thing. It would have dressed the next child in line I'm sure, while I would have been back in an old T-shirt. My hands are clamped together in front of me as if I am praying, my lips are pursed and I have a serious, conspiratorial look. You can see it's me though, despite the years. I don't like to look at it, but I force myself now.

"This is me," I tell her. She takes the photo between taloned forefingers and flicks it round for a better look. I see her brow furrow as she examines it. She looks up at me, and back at the photo. Then back at me. She breaks into a broad smile that flashes gold. She taps the photo.

"No," she says.

I hardly hear the rest of the interview for the booming of blood in my ears. When it is done, I walk blind from the orphanage, stumbling over clods of red earth. All I know is that I must get away from that place. I have to get away or the orphanage will pull me in through its doors and everything I have worked to become will be deleted and I will be returned to a small girl without a form or a connection to the world, poking in the earth with a stick. After all that hope, the records of my existence, and of my mother, said Woyzero Ayele, were lost to flood or termites. Perhaps they never kept them and she is making excuses. It doesn't matter anyway; the only thing that matters is that I know now that there is no way for me to find her. I will never know who she was. A chunk of my lost memories has been permanently excised; they have erased, lobotomised me. Why are you so angry? I demand of myself. Nothing has changed! For all those years you never wanted to know anyway!

I charge blindly from the building into the countryside.

That is just it. Nothing has changed and the relentlessness of my anger is killing me. I walk but I do not see; my chest is a rock and the breath has stopped at my throat to stop me screaming.

My eyes are dry with rage and injustice; I need to be alone to process this new loss – not just the loss of her, my fucking mother, but of myself. A stab to my heart reminds me what this means for the baby... I begin to run, holding myself together or I will fall apart. I stumble, head down, pushing through stands of eucalyptus and *enset*. They have ripped her from me. They, she, the woman who bore me, they have conspired to deprive me of any sense of wholeness I might ever know. In a sudden clearing I crouch on the nipped green velvet of the forest floor and before I let myself question what I am doing begin to dig. My nails attack the red soil, tearing at soil and roots and grit. I tear off the topsoil in chunks and rake my fingers into the earth below. I dig steadily. The earth is soft, though filled with stones. They wiggle free like loose teeth and I delve deeper. Deeper, deeper. I keep burrowing, intently, until my fingertips are raw and bleeding. Digging down into my past. I will finish what I started.

As I dig, I picture her little body in its yellow duckling fluff babygrow, now to be delivered to an orphanage as I was, because without knowing who and where I came from, how can I be a mother to her? I hold my heaving ribs to keep them from snapping open or with a crack they will deliver my heart and guts to the forest floor. I hurt all over; my head, my heart, my belly, but I keep digging. I dig for the child in me, the child in me that was abandoned. Is she under here? I don't know why I'm digging, but I know it is important. I dig with an angry irritation, digging into the great unhealed wound of my past with a dogged boredom so intense it numbs my mind. I have packed away my mother, drowned her with booze, anaesthetised her with narcotics, grappled her into submission and worked her to the ground, but I will never, never be free of the woman who deserted me, the space that she left.

I have made a hole in the turf now the size of my own body, just deep enough for me to lie in. My fingernails are broken and sharp bits of root and grit are embedded under my nails. There is no further to go. I have reached the bedrock, but it's OK. I am not making a grave for myself. I do not want to die. Quite the opposite.

I crawl on my knees into the shallow dent and turn over until I am lying on my back. There is a sharp stone under the back of my head and I turn over to wiggle it out and throw it aside. I shuffle myself back in and find I have done well. The shallow hole fits my body exactly. Here I am, packaged, contained, safe. The earth is cool but the sun is warm. I look up; above me the bluish-purple branches of the eucalyptus sway against a bright sky.

My head is empty. Empty of reason or plan or memory. For so many years I tried to catch a glimpse of my mother's face, but it has stayed stubbornly hidden in the locked box of my memories. Even now she won't meet my eye. Instead, I see T'irunesh, the mother of the baby. Her face, the hitched scar under one eye. Her fear, her astonishment. Somewhere out there, she is alone, carrying forever the guilt of her decision to abandon her child. Another half-person. I understand. Something in me shifts, softens. I let the earth take the weight of my body and I feel my anger draining into the rocks beneath me. I sleep.

It is quiet in the forest when I wake, so I hear the woman's soft footsteps before I see her. I startle and sit up in my earth bed, remembering where I am.

She is approaching along a narrow track. A local housewife, come to sweep up eucalyptus leaves for her small smoky fire. I try to arrange myself, pulling my knees up to my chest and turning my face away from her, but when I glance she is looking at me with wide steady eyes. Her face, lined with work and dirt and life, is tattooed at the throat and forehead with small crosses and she wears a black headscarf. She stares calmly, unruffled. Then, as she continues on her way, with a tiny tilt of her head she invites me to follow her.

I hesitate; I don't want to leave this place. I slept briefly but deeply and, on waking, my anger has dispersed and I feel lighter, hopeful somehow. Nothing has changed, and yet, subtly, everything has. It is a fragile, newborn feeling, and I must hold it close. I don't know if I am ready to present it to the world yet. However, looking around me, I have strayed so far from the path that I have no idea where I am. The woman has set off along a track, her back to me, her sack of leaves over her shoulder. I scramble upright and follow.

We walk. She does not turn. I watch her feet, dirty in their worn green jelly shoes, make soft small footsteps as I stumble clumsily after her. She walks fast. I wonder if I have misunderstood her gesture. Perhaps she thinks I am pursuing her. Perhaps she is afraid. I want to call out to reassure her, but I seem to have lost the ability to speak. We soon arrive at a small hut, surrounded by a makeshift fence of euphorbia and eucalyptus. A chicken and three chicks scratch in a pool of sunlight. She passes through the gate. I hesitate. She turns, still not smiling, but with an open face, and again, with a small tilt of her head, she signals follow.

I step into the darkness and sit on a low bed, a frame of woven cow hide covered in a blanket. The earthen floor is swept smooth, and in the centre of the room is a fireplace with a tiny spiral of smoke trickling up towards the rafters. My eyes begin to adjust.

The woman takes some dry leaves from her sack and adds them to the fire and blows. I watch blankly. I am glad of the darkness; I must look like a madwoman, covered in dirt, twigs in my hair. I have nothing to offer her, not even speech. I am a simpleton. The leaves crackle and the flames of the fire are mesmerising.

From a small pot, she takes a handful of green coffee beans and roasts them in a little metal pan over the flames and puts on water to boil. She does not speak but when they are roasted, brown and smoking, she proffers the pan to me, and I waft the fragrant smoke to my nostrils, a gesture of appreciation. It is rich and sharp and it brings me, one sense at a time, back into the world of the living. I watch as she crushes the beans in a mortar, and tips it into a black earthenware *jebena*. She places the coffee pot in the fire, and sits with me. Together we look into the flames.

As a teenager, when I was revising late into the night, my English mother would come and sit with me. She didn't need conversation, she didn't even bring a book to read, she was content to just be with me, to watch me. The Ethiopian woman sits with me in the same way my mother did. Accepting. She has little, but she is offering it freely, without expectation of thanks. Just like my mother did. Other women, widowed and left to care for a distressed toddler, not of their blood, a child who used to make her head bleed by banging it on the wall, a child who screamed all night to be held, might have run out of love. My mother never did.

Despite her loss, my mother gave me what she had. And it was enough. Despite everything, I *do* know what it is like to be loved and love in return. I have found my mother. Inside me. I *can* be a mother to the baby. And one day, perhaps my real mother, June, will meet her, and a stitch will be made, gathering up all the empty years, the gaping hole sewn shut. I will do a small good thing. I am enough. It will be enough.

The coffee pot is steaming and she takes it from the fire with a cloth and pours it into a small white cup. From the back of the hut she takes a tin, and spoons some of her precious sugar into it. Her fingers are calloused against the white china as she lifts it to me.

I sip the coffee; it is bittersweet, fiery, and it hits my stomach with a warmth that begins to saturate through me. By the time I have drained the cup to its grainy, sugary depths I am almost back in my body.

"*Ameseganallo*," I say, with a small, grateful smile. Thank you. She holds the look, her eyes glinting in the dark hut.

Tewodros

He is perturbed. His hostage is crying and cowering in the corner of his hut. He had not anticipated this excessive reaction. And he never intended to kidnap this baby.

When he saw the British midwife taking the cut-through up the side street near his hut, carrying a large bag and a bundle, he took it as a sign that it was time to take her. She did not see him hiding in the bushes, and he clamped his hand hard over her mouth before she could scream. He had to use all of his strength. She struggled, biting his fingers as he wrestled her through the low door, and when he released her, she scrabbled over to the corner, panting and making a fuss. It was only then that he realised she was not Mariam, not the one he wanted, but another nurse, an Ethiopian one that looked like her.

The emperor will be disappointed in him. He made a mistake. On the other hand, the baby is a bonus, of a kind. A bargaining point. He has been sitting looking at the child for some hours now. The light is beginning to dim in the small room and he will have to use one of the precious candles. The nurse keeps pleading with him to let them both go, says she needs to take the child to the orphanage or back to the hospital; he is fed up with her snivelling. She is one of the common people. She is not strong. He must be patient, but really she is testing him.

At first he tried to show her that he would not harm her.

He left the glass shard he was holding by the door and came closer, reaching in his pocket for gum. But she wailed and exhorted him not to rape her. She whimpered and clutched the child so close to her that it began to yell. He told her to make it quiet, so from the cool bag she was carrying the nurse produced a bottle of milk, which it guzzled like a snorting piglet before falling asleep. He would like to let this woman go, but he does not know how to care for the child. He could feed it, but there are things like dirty cloths to change and he does not want to handle the child alone.

She tells him that she has a phone. If he allows her, she will call whoever he wants and tell them what his demands are.

"Call the English woman."

She is confused.

"The English nurse. Mariam," he says.

Her eyes widen, but she searches her phone for the number. It is no surprise to him that this random woman with a passing similarity to Mariam should have the number for exactly his intended captive in her phone. No, it shows the divine plan of his operation. He smiles, squatting on his haunches and gesturing her to ring. The woman calls with shaking hands.

"Mariam. Are you there? Are you back in Addis? Where? Bole? Thank God. You must come. I can't speak. I have the baby here. I'm near the hospital, just behind, on the cut-through on the way to Kera. Yes, I was taking her to the orphanage. Yes, Tadesse ordered it. He said it was time. Mariam, wait, I had no choice. But listen, listen! We've been—" The nurse grits her teeth and makes a gurning noise through her frozen jaws, a noise like childbirth, before she masters her fear and composes herself. "Taken. I don't know who he is. A man. Yes, kidnapped. He wants you to come. He says he knows you. No, I don't know his name." She glances up, with round eyes.

He thinks carefully, then speaks emphatically in English so that Mariam will understand.

"A person."

"He says he's... a person."

There is a silence on the other end before the reply comes. The nurse hangs up.

"She says she is coming."

He nods, and leans back against the wall to wait.

When Mariam comes, she comes alone. That is good. He sees her loitering on the road, under the single broken lamp post. Her face looks gaunt. He will offer her a banana. There will be time for police and politicians later, but he would like to speak with her before all that distraction. He was too shy before, but now that the emperor speaks to him, through him, and he has the confidence, indeed the obligation, to speak with her, for it is she who will carry his messages.

The exchange happens smoothly. It is too dark to see her face, but he gestures to her from the doorway and she makes her way up to the shack; she does not look at him. Her face is a stern mask. He holds open the corrugated iron and she steps in. Only then does she break; she rushes to the nurse and the baby and holds them. She checks the baby over, asking questions in English and kissing the child's face. It moves its small hands and she kisses those too.

"Did you call the police?" says the nurse, under her breath.

The midwife glances sharply at him, and sees that he understands.

"No," she says, for his benefit. "No police. It's too risky. Let me talk to him. I know him a little. I need to handle this myself."

He smiles, and holds open the corrugated iron door and gestures for the first nurse to leave. She looks uncertain.

"Go," says the foreigner. He sees her expression; it conveys, 'Get help'.

The nurse nods and moves feebly to the doorway. He shows her his broken-glass weapon as she leaves, as a reminder that he has some power. Her face is horrified.

"Don't hurt them," she whimpers.

He is astonished. Of course not.

She staggers out into the night and he is left with the foreigner and the baby.

Mariam has wedged herself into a corner, the baby in its blankets bundled in her arms. He remembers the banana. It is a little blackened but still good. He offers it to her. She shakes her head. He will have to think of another way to put her at her ease.

"We will not hurt you," he tells her in soft English. "They would not listen, so we had to take you." He delves into his bag, bringing out a grimy piece of paper. "Read, please. You will understand."

She takes the paper from him, turns it towards to the candle light and reads.

St George. George Washington. Washing machine Moscow Omo Belgium chewing gum Mitsubishi Mosque Afro motors magic carpet meskel Allah is good to me. Hawassa NASA Internet Winternet Wayne Rooney Yuri Gagarin Germany Manufacture SOS an international distress signal. Stephen Segal Fire Down below   Shola Milk for health Total "Dimple"

> *Coffee shop Abebe Ethiopia Red Cross ambulance service Embassy of Belgium Gum tree chewing gum Diabetes honey bees Moenco car repair Moenco Moon Omo washing powder Omo valley SOS children's villages Embassy of the Czech Republic Christian Aid-we believe in life before death. German. Mango juice. Top rack of dishwasher only. Not to be used in microwave. Made in China. Virgin Mary. WEATHER-harvest, wheat Nile Insurance TOTAL Voice of America. Suarez. Liverpool. Jesus died for me. Not to be sold or exchanged. Not to be sold or exchanged. Not to be sold or exchanged.*

He points enthusiastically to the words, rummaging for more sheets. She examines them one by one. He can see that she understands their significance. For what are things but an external expression of the world, a surface skin beneath which lies deeper meaning? The words are a clarion cry, a representation of the state of the nation. She will understand. She nods at him, encouragingly. Dare he show her his list of commandments?

He keeps it now in a safe place, hidden in the eaves of the shack. He has wrapped it reverently, as befits its importance, in crackly gold paper. The paper has *Happy Birthday* printed on it, but it is all he could find. One day it will have its own case in the National Museum, or perhaps it will be locked in a vault, guarded by a single priest like the Arc of the Covenant at Axum. He brings it down and spreads it out on the floor before her. She leans over the sleeping child to read the words. He feels the still, the gathering of energy. George the Father, George the Son, George the Holy Ghost. He feels the emperor in him, waiting for her reaction, his nostrils flaring like a great stallion, ready to kick or rear, ready to gallop across the mountain ridge. He wishes his head did not throb so. The eye nearest the candle sees well, but a dark disc obscures the other side of his vision; he shakes his head, and places a palm over that eye.

"Are you ill?" she asks.

He shakes his head in irritation. Did she not read the words? Was she not profoundly affected by their wisdom? Pah. Perhaps he should not have expected her to understand them; they were never meant for a woman. After all, a woman can never aspire to be a real man. He should have tested her further before trusting her with the knowledge of his scroll. Perhaps she is one of those misguided females who think women are equal to men. Emperor Tewodros rears back, assessing her with an arrogant eye and he, himself, feels the anger of disappointment rise in him. He sneers at her, hisses, and snatches back the list. She whimpers, shrinking back. After a few moments, with bowed head, she speaks. Her voice is small and shocked.

"It is very powerful," she says. "This list is very important to you."

"It is *the list*," he says proudly as he stows it away once more. "What it says, must be."

She nods.

"It is George's list," he confides.

She looks confused.

"George?" she whispers.

He smiles indulgently and whispers, "George Bush. He is my master."

Her face in the candlelight is aghast. He sees that the man's name itself can strike fear into her. After a few moments, she finds her voice.

"Well, we should definitely make sure that people see this

list. Perhaps I can take it to people who can help you," she offers, unsure.

"Yes, yes," he says, pleased that she has understood so quickly. The emperor is pleased too. He can feel his noble heart moving beneath his own shirt. She will be useful to the cause after all. She was a good choice. He has done well.

But she continues, "I can get you help. There are people who can help you. Good people. Kind people. I'll make sure that they treat you well. But you need to let me go, and the baby. She's been sick for many months. She needs to be in a safe place. Please, let me go and I promise I'll find help for you."

He shakes his head. This cannot be allowed. She has missed the point. She is making him angry again.

He fixes her with a firm look.

"They are like Philistines who attacked David, but we shall conquer. A great king will come."

They are the emperor's words. He delivers them in flawless unaccented English. Although it is night he feels the ray of sunlight that bathed him as he stood reciting in the classroom over a decade ago. The emperor inside him throws back his head and laughs in recognition, and at his audacity.

She is astonished, but she manages to mutter, "You must let us go. There is not enough milk for this baby. By tomorrow it will all be gone. Please."

He feels suddenly ashamed, meek and uncertain behind his bravado. He takes himself to a far corner and rocks. The pain in his head is increasing. He is used to bearing such things, but the emperor is disgusted with his weakness; he makes a fist with one hand and begins to smack and grind it into his open palm. On the other side of the room, the nurse cowers. Perhaps he is not the best vehicle for such an illustrious man as the emperor; the duality threatens to split him, to burst his head like an overripe watermelon.

Time passes. They do not speak. The noises of the city lessen, and there are no cars on Roosevelt. He finds the silence oppressive. He gets up and goes outside to urinate; Venus shines bright and blue in the night sky, but one side of his vision is starless and black. Time is running out. He re-enters the shack to find her fumbling with her mobile phone.

"Yes, near Kera. Rahel knows where. Don't do anything to frighten him. Stay back unless you hear me shout. John, no police, OK?"

He lunges towards her with a roar and grabs the phone from her hand. She gives up her mobile without a struggle, thrusting it at him with hands up, palms out. He raises a cautionary finger to her. If they are to come, it will be on his terms, not hers.

And now Tewodros wants to pace, so he must follow. *The king's heart is in the hand of the lord. Like the rivers of water, he turns it wherever he wishes.* He moves from one side of the room to the other, lamenting his lack of resources, his lack of influence. He has been misunderstood for so long and this was to be his moment of triumph. You can never rely on others. He should have waited, bided his time, trusted in the superiority of his position rather than acting so rashly, before trusting to foreign influence.

There is an insidious whisper in his ear: the voice of Tewodros's paranoia and self-pity. It is pernicious and unsettling. When he can ignore it no longer, he looks inwards to address his master directly; he finds the emperor ablaze and feverish.

"Take the baby from her. Then they will listen."

He stops, stilled by the instruction. This was not part of the plan.

"What should I do?" he whispers.

The foreigner has risen to her feet. She clutches the baby, but she looks ready to fight if he tries to take it.

He moves towards the broken glass, and takes it in his hand, but he is afraid that the emperor will direct him towards things he is not capable of.

"Take the baby. Make a sacrifice. Spill its blood."

The emperor is grinding his teeth, but Tewodros, the man Tewodros, hesitates. If he does this, they *will* listen. They *will* take him seriously. The emperor's logic is infallible, and yet... He turns, retreats to the far side of the room and drops the shard of glass in disgust. Something wicked has come over the emperor; something animal. He must silence this train of thought before the emperor's blood-fury overwhelms him. He prays the emperor will forgive him for what he is about to do. With the full force of his strength he strikes the emperor full in the face.

Tewodros stumbles, then sits down wearily. His jaw hurts where the punch fell. Before the police come, before the television cameras arrive, he will have to make peace with the emperor, to channel his fearsome manliness into a language that can speak to the world. He wishes his head did not ache. The baby begins to cry, and now the foreigner cries too.

"Shh," he entreats. And then more roughly, "Please shut up."

Dr Tadesse

It is the end of his shift and he is writing notes. The first he hears of it is when Rahel runs into the ward and takes his hand and pulls him from his office out into the corridor. Her hair is wild and she can hardly speak. She has clearly been crying. When she finally manages to gasp out her news, he sets off at a run, taking the stairs two at a time with his long legs, hearing her clatter, sobbing, behind him. The patients stare; those who have gathered on the landings mutter and confer while the feeble stand with open mouths as he rushes past.

I will never forgive myself, he thinks. And the administration will never forget. His white coat flaps behind him as he sprints out of the hospital compound and into the dark street. A taxi swerves to avoid him, the driver shouting abuse, but he runs across the road without thought for his own safety.

"The child is medically well. It is time for her to leave. We are a hospital, are we not?" he had told Rahel when he ordered her to take the child to the orphanage. He'd had enough of waiting for the police to come to collect her. "Today is the day!" He'd told her triumphantly, then ruined it by glancing over his shoulder in case Mariam had unexpectedly returned. "I'm not hard-hearted, Rahel," he had explained when she protested. He could tell she thought him a coward, but what would she know of the responsibility of his position? He gave her money to take a taxi. Why did she walk, the little fool?

He is running hard, but Rahel shouts for him to stop and

he pulls up, at the entrance of the cut-through, half expecting it to be already full of police. The cut-through is quiet. A single flickering street lamp shows him the location of the shack. If the hospital management hear of how he did not follow the proper procedure, but arranged for the baby to be moved, he will be for it, but that is the least of his worries. The baby is an issue but one of his nurses, and now a foreign midwife kidnapped? What is she even doing in Addis? She was meant to be in Sidama. He realises he does not have a plan and he has not even called the police yet.

"Dr, Dr..." pants Rahel, holding on to his sleeve, "don't do anything. He may harm them. We have to be careful! Mariam said no police, not until she had talked to him!"

She is bug-eyed. God knows what this crazy character has done to her. He has a sudden rush of pity and regrets that he ever had lascivious thoughts about her. She is a girl, and this is partly his fault. Partly.

"I will talk to him," he says boldly. "Is he big? I could overwhelm him. I am tall."

"No!" she insists. "He only wants to talk to Mariam. He knows her somehow. We may need you, if the baby gets hurt. And I think we should call John."

"John? Why? What can he do that I can't?" sneers the doctor, pulling himself up to his fullest height.

"I don't mean that... It's just that he and Mariam, they, I think, well, all the nurses have been discussing it. I think he would want to know."

So he was right about the good doctor and the stubborn midwife. It seems unimportant now.

"No. He'll be too emotional. He might do something stupid. We should call the police. They will know what to do."

He wants to devolve responsibility, let the people trained

for this kind of thing take over. After his sprint his lungs are scorched and his muscles shaking. He pulls out his phone, but the nurse grabs it from his hand.

"The police will bring guns and scare him. You know what they are like. They would not listen. It will be crazy, lights and noise and someone will surely get hurt. Mariam said she'd met this man before. He did seem to respond to her. Maybe we should just wait."

The nurse's suggestion is inadequate, but he doesn't have a better one.

They stand on the corner like two lovers feeling ridiculous; his impotence in the situation is making him more and more angry. After a while he realises she is trembling with cold so he offers her his white coat and a toffee from his top pocket. It is the little things. Perhaps he can atone with the little things.

There is a screeching of tyres and a white Land Cruiser pulls up at the end of the road. A figure runs into the cut-through and stands disorientated, looking for a direction.

"John, here!" calls Rahel in a low voice and he scrambles over to them.

"Where is she?" His voice is hoarse. He is in shirt sleeves and jeans. "She rang. She said she's in a hut somewhere. Do you know where she is? What happened?"

Rahel tells him and he lets out a low noise like a sob. He collects himself.

"Did he hurt you, Rahel?"

She shakes her head.

He pulls at his hair, pacing in the shadows.

"What do we do?" he asks Tadesse, their differences forgotten.

The Ethiopian claps two strong hands on the foreigner's shoulders to hold him still.

"We must wait," he says.

"But what if he hurts her? We have to do something," John hisses in reply.

Tewodros

It is coming. The fit of all fits. He can feel its arrival like the low rumble of thunder that presages rain. He knew a fit would come, but this feels bigger than any he has known before. As it builds, his head throbs and searing nerve pains flash down the left side of his body. He dreads it, wants it. When it comes, it will bring relief. Perhaps it will bring inspiration.

The demands of the emperor have intensified; his own thoughts are obliterated by the monarch's theorising, his truculence, his need for action. The woman's eyes are fixed, but every now and then he sees her lurch into sleep, then rouse herself. He didn't mean to frighten her, snatching the phone off her like that. But she had to know who is in charge. The baby has drunk its last bottle of milk and seems peaceful. Will it remember this adventure? He hopes not. He is sorry it was ever brought into this.

He places the shard of glass into a corner where it will not harm him if he thrashes, as he has been told he does. It is a shame that the fit is coming before they have had a chance to get to know each other; he would have liked to discuss things further with Mariam, to ask her all the questions he had prepared, but when it came to it he found that his English was not so adept as he thought, and she kept returning to her theme of seeking help for him. Perhaps when they have parted ways she will become a disciple and disseminate his words, his lists. He makes sure that he is between her and the door. He has not the time or energy to tie her up. If she chooses to run, she will have to get past him, and though he cannot stop her he feels that the sight of him fitting will deter her at least.

He sinks to his knees as it comes on but the sensation is one of rising. The pain behind his eye recedes and he has sight again. The breeze lifts him upwards, and he soars like a ragged raven up to his hill top. Far below he sees the toytown of Addis Ababa, the insignificance of his little refuge. He sweeps, then, up country, over the brown hills, the pink earth. The green valleys are bathed in sunlight now and the true plenty of the land is revealed. And he is lord over it. He is Tewodros, and this is his heritage, his destiny. He is so proud. A faint smudge of cloud hovers below the long flat ridge of the Amba. Meqdella; he has arrived. The defining moment is drawing closer.

He sees his troops amassed in ranks on the hill top and there in the middle, his great gun, Sebastopol. As he descends to the earth his soldiers let out a resounding cheer; Amhar fighters, Oromos, Afar warriors, Gurage Muslims; he has brought together all the men of Ethiopia, in equality, in unity. A face in the crowd is familiar; the broad grin and jug ears of his own father, back from the dead to fight for his son. His father holds his gun aloft and smiles shyly at Tewodros; his son's eyes fill with tears but he salutes the older man. He feels the warm flood of forgiveness pass between them. "A real man knows the importance of family," he says in a low voice, finally understanding the last item on the list.

Just then, onto the ridge prances a fabulous palomino pony. He gasps and clasps his heart. On its back, handsome, square-jawed, muscular, is George Bush, the former president of the

United States of America. He canters towards Tewodros and when he reaches him he bows low. From his jibbing pony he offers Tewodros a hand. Hesitant, Tewodros takes it. The American's hand is so soft, so smooth. Tewodros looks with satisfaction at his black hand clasping the white. This was what he wanted all along; dignity. He throws his head back and laughs and the president smiles with him, showing his perfect white teeth.

They hear the *tantantara* of a military bugle and over the crescent of the hill a cavalry of American Confederate soldiers come riding with blond hair, silver buckles and spurs shining. One leads a fabulous white stallion for Tewodros to mount. He leaps, swings his leg over it and sits firm in the saddle, feeling the horse hot and excitable between his thighs. It is time.

A man on an Oromo pony canters up and offers him binoculars. His heart quails when he sees the Eritrean army marching upon them, their soldiers bristling with grenades. He adjusts the binoculars and he sees that one entire platoon is composed of glue-sniffing boys, their parrot hair rigid, caked with ochre and defiance. Among the enemy he sees another squadron of Gurkhas, led by General Napier, their breech-loading Sniders ready to fell his cavalry like before.

This time, though, he has a proper army. The game is equal. He nods to a soldier, who lets out a sharp blast on his trumpet.

"To death or glory!" yells Tewodros.

The Confederate army, the Gurages, the Oromos and the Amhars, the whole band let out such a noise that the entire mountaintop shakes.

Almost immediately the battle is upon them and it is wonderful. The air is filled with the smell of cordite and sweat. The horse beneath him wants to race and run; he lets it gallop a wide arc, leading the way for his army, leading by example. In his hands is a silver scimitar bequeathed him by some past ruler. He slashes it as he gallops, scoring open the bellies of glue-sniffers as he races by. He feels no remorse. His father rides alongside him now, reinless, shouldering a rifle. *Pop pop pop* – three Eritreans are felled. They turn back together, keeping pace at a gallop, laughing wildly.

They draw up near Sebastopol and leap from their ponies to watch the joyful carnage from the safe shadow of the gun. Across the field, General Napier, his walrus moustache bristling, is commanding his Gurkhas from behind, mounted on an elephant. Suddenly, through the smoke, they see a horse; it is charging straight at the Englishman. On its back is George W. Bush, naked to the waist, swinging a cutlass around his head. Napier balks as the horse comes on, but George has already thrown himself upon the elephant, clambered up its side and is upon him. The general's red mouth is a horrible 'O' beneath his drooping moustache as his head flies from his body. The president pushes the corpse off the elephant and stands triumphant on its back.

Yet still the enemy come. They swarm up the hillside now like cockroaches, picking off his golden boys, his glorious compatriots, and flinging them to the bottom of the cliff. Dread and destiny rise in him. The tide has turned and his army are faltering, falling. The air is full of acrid smoke and he hears the *ack-ack-ack* of strafing gunfire, the sound of men and horses screaming. He knows the hour is close when he must play his final card; he must fire the great gun, Sebastopol.

He is alone; he had not understood that he would face the moment alone, but now it comes he knows that it is right. He embraces the cannon, laying his body against the impersonal metal and feeling the world's indifference in its steel. The gun, pregnant with death and destruction, has chilled in the shadow of the battle smoke and seems to draw the heat from him. The gun is loaded with his hopes and fears. So much pride packed into its grey body; so much at stake. It may not survive the firing. He takes a flint from his pocket and strikes a spark that sets the fuse alight with a blue sizzle. He watches the fuse burn down with the detached fascination of a man about to die.

The great gun explodes; a tsunami of dark blood rolls across Meqdella, sweeping the armies, both defenders and attackers, into the abyss. Horses, soldiers and elephants, the ex-president of the United States, all are engulfed by the tide of black liquid and their battle noises silenced. Tewodros too is rolling, caught in a blood-breaker that turns him this way and that, carrying him over the *amba* into the blood-flooded valley. He struggles for breath, thrashing as his lungs fill with the sticky liquid. With the firing of the gun, the aneurysm, the bulge of blood that has been slowly forming in the vessels of his brain, ruptures with the relief of pent-up waters flooding from a broken dam. Both sides of his vision darken now, but small explosions in his synapses fill the waters with twinkling light. He watches them, marvelling. It is surprisingly peaceful to die and he is not lonely. *Open my eyes, that I may see marvellous things.* The world is beautiful; he has always thought so. Finally he stops struggling, submits, and follows the lights into the great darkness.

Mariam

It takes me a while to understand what is happening. At first he seems to slump, then his whole body goes rigid and starts to twitch and tremor like electric shocks are moving through it. Of course I have seen epileptic fits before, but I'm not expecting him to have one right now. I didn't realise he had epilepsy. It's unexpected; another weird and horrific assault on us. I pull myself into the corner and hug the baby closer. The fit goes on and on; the muscles of his face pull tight and his eyes flick open; they roll back in his head, showing white. I could get away; make a run for it, but he is in front of the door, the shard of glass beyond him. I keep preparing to launch myself, but the moment isn't right. I can't get a sure enough grip on the baby; what if he grabs my ankle and I drop her? The fit consumes him; his heels beat on the wooden floor rhythmically like a child having a tantrum; his fists are up at his chest as if he were holding an invisible dumbbell. His breath hisses out from between his teeth, which are clenched so tight his jaw bulges.

Then suddenly it all stops.

His whole body loosens and unclenches. His head falls sideways and I startle to see that his eyes are open and he is staring right at me. A long slow breath seeps out of him; there is a rattle to it. His face is soft, mild. Forgiving. A slight smile on his lips. Christ taken from the cross. I am holding my breath. I take a small gulp and let it out in a shaky stream.

The seconds pass and still he doesn't speak. Then I see. There is no movement in his chest. He is not breathing.

Without considering what I am about to do I put the baby down in her bundle of blankets and move quickly over to him. The first thing I do is take the shard of glass and throw it into a pile of refuse where he will not see it if he wakes. Then I pick up his warm limp hand and feel for a pulse. Nothing. No breath. I go into procedure. Professional. I know how to do this. I tip back his head to clear his airway, part his lips to check the position of his tongue. Then I pinch his nose, hold his chin and place my mouth over his and began CPR.

Two breaths. Thirty pumps to the heart. His body is frail under the layers of clothes he wears. Chest like a bird. Malnourished. How old is he? I'd thought him maybe forty but I see he is young, not even thirty under the grime and grizzled beard. I breathe through my mouth; the smell of him makes me gag and I have to pause to control myself. His fine beard brushes my chin as the air from my lungs enters his chest. I want to call him by his name, to bring him back to his body, but he's never told me his name.

"Come on, come on. That's it, breathe. Take a breath. It's OK, you can do it," I insist. And I do want him to come back. To tell him how angry I am with him. To smooth things over. To forgive him. I won't press charges. I'll get him help; I have a colleague in psychiatric services who could get him meds, counselling maybe. "Come on, you bastard, breathe," I hiss as I pump away at his heart. My arms are getting tired; I can feel the build-up of lactic acid in my muscles; when I am in the breathing cycle, they shake. I can't do this for much longer. The adrenalin, the lack of sleep. I am exhausted.

If I call out for help, they will drag me away from him. They will not understand how I could want to save my captor, why I wouldn't want him dead after all he's done to us. So I must get him breathing before I shout. Somewhere in the backstreets, waiting, must be John and Rahel. They've come alone, I hope. But even John might not understand my mad desire to save this man. I can't afford the risk. I must act now.

I keep pumping. Ten, twenty cycles. But it is too late. He is already gone. I sit back on my heels and wipe my mouth. He is smiling at the ceiling.

"I'm sorry," I say, and I feel the tears come. "I'm sorry."

I lean over to him, and place a hand on his chest. With the other I touch his face. I wonder where his mother is, if she remembers the son she bore and birthed. His face already has the cast of death; the slip of the cheeks and jaw, the eyes settling back into their sockets for their long sleep. I slide a palm over his eyelids and pull them down. Then I put my head on his chest and cry silently, so as not to wake the child. I am not crying only for him. I am crying for myself, for what I have just been through and for the sadness and futility of life.

I sit up and wipe a string of snot from my nose. The baby is stirring, but she doesn't cry yet. I know there are people who love me nearby. I know they are worried and waiting, but I need to sit with his body for just a while before I leave him. I am not ready to relinquish him to the cold morgue yet. He owes me this time for what he did to us, and I owe it to him to accompany him for this short while. Whatever else he was, he was a human being; our lives touched, passing through. In some way I will never understand I meant something to him; across the distance of our separate lives we connected with each other.

I wonder about the list he showed me, about the plan he spoke of and what it meant. I wonder where his life went wrong. I'll never know. I didn't know him well enough and now I never will.

I admire him, in a way. For doing something. For taking on the vast shittiness of his world and refusing to accept it. We all need a plan. He did something. Not the right thing perhaps, but he did something. There is consolation in action. Perhaps his list helped him to make sense of the world. He wanted to be remembered, to be part of history. Some good it brought him. His mistake was to think that we could change everything. We can't. But we can change something. A small good thing, John said.

The candle flickers and goes out, but the room is not dark. Without my knowing it, the dawn has risen. The deep blue of the sky gives enough light to see by. A tiny slant of moon hangs in the sky. I put out a hand to touch his cheek. His skin has grown cold.

He is passing into stories. Perhaps he would have liked that. To have the lineage of story when there is no one to remember you, when your movement through time has left no mark of your passage. He will become words, my words. My breath in his lungs. Someone once told me that the cells from your mother's milk stay alive in your body for the rest of your life. My mother is in me and my breath is in his lungs. He is my brother, my son. We are connected. I do not know the stories of my own childhood, but I will tell people about him. I will tell the baby her story and she will ask for it again and again, until together we will tell it to her children. It is the only thing that makes sense, passing on the story of our blood and our love.

The baby starts to whimper. She has kicked aside the blanket and is lying in her yellow duckling babygrow. She is no longer the skinny wisp she was, she's sturdier. Healthy.

Stiffly I unfold my legs and move over to her. I lift her out of the blankets. She is rooting and hungry, but I meet her eye and say hello. She clocks me and her small mouth makes a shape like an 'o' and then, quite miraculously, her lips move apart into a twisted smile. She is seven weeks old and it is her first and she has gifted it to me. I bring her towards me and kiss her warm cheeks and feel her soft skin next to mine. She sucks at my face hungrily; it makes me laugh and I bring her to me and smell her head, the sweet essence of her. I burrow my nose into her curls.

Through the plastic tarpaulin at the window I see the sun has risen. I gather up her blanket and the cool bag. Respectfully we move around the body of our captor, and step out into a new morning.

The baby

The baby is excited. There are new colours in her world; someone has placed a toy in her cot and she is trying to reach it. She cannot coordinate her arms and legs, but her attempts sometimes bring her hand into contact with the plush fabric. The toy is a penguin, and she is excited by the contrast between its black and white. She would like to mouth it, to feel the fibres on her tongue. Her mouth is her world; she tastes and tests everything, extends her pink tongue, brings her small fists up to her mouth; this gives her a sense of herself, it is her ability to soothe herself when she is alone. But she has not been alone much in the last few days.

Since the return to hospital, her world has been full of noise and variety. She has been examined by several doctors who shone lights in her eyes, listened to her chest and took her temperature. During her waking hours, she and the woman have spent a lot of time looking into each other's eyes. She watches the woman's face, following her expressions, letting them guide her own. When she sees the woman respond to her own expressions, she grows intent. She is enthralled, in her own agency, in the woman, in herself. She feels herself, and yet she feels at one with the woman. She is never sure who is leading or following.

Mostly though she has been resting, next to the woman's warm body. It smells right, this body; the sharp reek of sweat and adrenaline disappeared after the first day and she felt the muscles slowly soften. There has been a lot of talk and many voices have come and gone.

She tires of the toy. Grizzles softly, sucks her fist and sleeps. While she sleeps, she is lifted. She brings her knees up briefly, folding herself close to the woman's body. Then slowly, reassured by the rhythmic pump-sluice of her heart, she adjusts herself to its soft contours.

"Why did you go? You should have told someone. Mariam, he could have killed you. He could have killed you both." The voice is male, husky, overwrought, but the woman is calm.

"I know. But I didn't believe he would. And I had to go to her. You understand, don't you? I couldn't risk not going."

"I thought you were going to die. When I heard him shouting into the phone."

"I'm sorry, John. I'm sorry."

"No. Don't, don't. You're here. You're safe."

The door swings open. The baby feels her carer stiffen. She jerks her head. Another louder voice speaks. She does not like this voice and she cannot tell the reason for its loudness. There is no correlation of volume and tone and it disconcerts her. She scrabbles at the woman's chest with her sharp nails. Turns her head away.

"Mariam. John. We thank God that you have been returned safe to us, Mariam. We were all so worried."

"Thank you, Dr Tadesse. It has been a shock to us all, but we are back now."

"I myself ran the whole way from the hospital. I was ready to take on this madman if need be. It was Rahel who persuaded me that it would not be in the best interests of the baby. It's true John, isn't it? We had to both hold back our desire to overwhelm this individual."

"It was good advice, Tadesse. It was wise to wait."

"How is Rahel?" asks the woman.

"Rahel? She is well. I have told her to take sick leave, but she tells me she wants to come back as soon as possible. She wants to see Mariam and the baby," says the man.

The woman sighs.

"Please give her our love. And please say sorry. It was me he wanted, not her. I'm sorry she was involved."

"I will tell her. Mariam, there is something else."

"What?"

"The police came today to collect the baby."

The woman starts and sits upright. The baby is squeezed so tight that she lets out a sharp squeak of protest.

"No! I won't let them. I'm not going to give her up! You can't make me. Tadesse, I beg you, please, you have to speak to them, please."

"Mariam, Mariam, shh. I told them she is still under observation and we have no plans to discharge her. We will keep her here for as long as you want. They didn't care. The orphanage has many other babies to fill its beds, after all. We'll make room for you here too, if you want to stay."

"Thank you, Tadesse. I'm sorry to cause you so much trouble. I won't forget this."

The doctor coughs in embarrassment.

"As long as you need."

The door opens and closes and there is silence.

"He didn't have to do that," the woman says.

"He's a good man."

"Hmm. Perhaps."

"He's going to have a lot of explaining to do to the administration but he'll come out of this OK."

The baby feels a large rough hand cup her skull. She reaches out, grabs a finger and pulls it to her mouth. It tastes of warm salt. She likes the taste. It is familiar. There is a long silence. The baby sucks thoughtfully on the finger, feeling the short nail press against the roof of her mouth, the rough whorls of its finger pad against her tongue.

"I need her, John. I need her more than anything," says the woman finally.

"Yes."

"What if they don't let me adopt her? I'll go mad."

"Why wouldn't they let you? You've saved her life many times over. You know her better than anyone. Look at her, how relaxed she is."

"But... I'm a foreigner. A foreigner whose visa is soon going to run out."

The baby sucks on, listening to the silence, waiting for the rumbling answer. It doesn't come for a long while.

"Let me help you."

"How?"

Mariam

That night, Rahel comes in to do a shift. She's meant to be off work, but she tells me she'll sleep with the baby near her all night so I can get some rest. I kiss the sleeping child, soaking up as much as I can of her sweet features, the way her long lashes brush against her cheek.

When I leave her, I feel an aching hole in my chest, an anxiety that can only be soothed by touching her, holding her. I think of the two holes I dug in the Sidama earth to hold and contain me. She does that for me now, filling me from inside. When I take her out of the hospital, she will need a name. I will find her the most beautiful name in the world.

As I emerge from the ward I find John. He is asleep in an uncomfortable chair, his head on his arms. He reminds me of the fathers in the lobby outside; their lives on hold, waiting for news. I realise he has not left the hospital since we were admitted. I place a hand on his arm and he starts awake. He peers at me through one half-open eye and flashes me a grin; we walk together to his car without speaking.

It's a clear night and a sliver of moon hangs over Addis Ababa. The streets are empty but for the packs of trotting dogs. We drive slowly up Churchill, past Sebastopol. The gun metal gleams in the car headlights. I think of the man who held us captive, the man who wanted to be Tewodros. When the hospital releases his body, when enquiries have been made, when, perhaps, some of his family have been found, we will bury him. I want to get him out of the morgue. That place of incongruous strangers, housed in strange intimacy; I want to hurry him out of that loveless waiting room and into the warm earth. Up on Yeka, at the church on the hill, perhaps, if they will accept him there. John's Ethiopian father knows the priest. I want there to be a place we can visit, so we can continue the conversation that his death cut short. A one-sided conversation I know, but I have not done with him yet. I will hold him for a while longer.

Tibs, greets us at the door, mewling. John's housekeeper has been feeding her, but she's missed him. She winds herself around his legs and even consents to a stroke from me.

John looks exhausted. I used to think he was like an owl, all stiff feathers and a hard beak. Untouchable. I was wrong. He's softer than that. We've shaken him up, me and the baby. I want to take him in my arms and hold him, but I don't dare. Things are too precarious.

I shower while he makes tea. The hot water is wonderful, and I soap myself all over, scrubbing at my flesh, luxuriating in the smoothness of my body. I wash my hair with his shampoo and I step out of the shower smelling masculine and energised. In his bathroom cabinet (electric razor, paracetamol, nail clippers) I find a hotel toothbrush, still in its wrapper, and brush my teeth. In the mirror, I hardly recognise myself. I look thinner, nervous; there is a furrow between my eyebrows that I don't remember. But there is a clarity too; an openness. I wonder if I haven't been wearing a mask all these years. I quite like the person I find underneath it. I put on his dressing gown and wonder where I will be sleeping tonight.

We drink our tea quietly, sitting together at the kitchen table. Outside, in the cedar forest that rises up behind John's house, the hyenas are whooping to the night sky. It is time. I push back my teacup, and take his hand. It is cool, tanned and freckled, blond hairs. I turn it in mine; short blunt nails, long fingers. He submits to my examination with his pale blue eyes trained on me. I stroke up one forearm, feeling the dry roughness of his skin, skin damaged in childhood by the strong African sun. I turn one palm upwards. What do the creases mean? Where do I figure in the pattern on his skin? I move up his arm, thumbing blue veins, pale milky skin, a smattering of small freckles. Despite my exhaustion, I'm breathless with my need to touch him. I lift up a hand to his face. His eyes are wide, pupils dark with what... fear? Desire? I trace the pattern of worry lines on his forehead and he closes his eyes. I smooth the creases on his skin that mark the length of his life, all his struggles, all his joys. I want to hear the stories they tell. I need to stroke smooth what we have inflicted on him, the baby and me. I brush his cheek with the lightest touch of one finger; it moves over his blond stubble and my finger burns as if it were a match set alight on his skin.

"Mariam?" he asks. His voice is low and unsure. I nod. He squeezes my hand and pulls me up so we are both standing. Then, very carefully, he takes my head in his hands. I close my eyes and feel his warmth approaching. His mouth is gentle on mine; it is almost an effort to retract the smile that has formed on my lips but I begin to respond to his kisses. Tentative at first, then deeper. I release into them, gripping a handful of his hair and drinking him in. My hands are on him, feeling the solid presence of him, and he in turn pulls me closer, until the whole length of our bodies is touching. He's hard, I can feel him against my belly. The long corridor to the bedroom is a boundary of sorts, and we know that we must cross it together. Unwilling to let go of each other we stumble comically, still kissing, towards the bedroom.

"John, I want you." My words are stifled by his mouth on mine, his warm open mouth. We collapse on his bed. He rolls me over on my back, his weight on top of me, pushing his head into my neck and kissing up my throat, then moving down to the opening of the dressing gown I am wearing.

"Mariam, Mariam, Mariam!" he groans. "You are so..."

I put my finger to his lips and roll him sideways so now it is him lying on his back. I want to freeze-frame this moment, stop time so I can explore him at my leisure. I will replay this scene; I want to savour it. Very slowly I begin to undo the top buttons of his shirt, feeling the spring of the hair on his chest against my fingers as I go. I slide my hand inside, brushing my palms against the hardness of his nipples. He is holding his breath. Slowly I continue to unbutton his shirt until finally I reach his belly. He bites his lip as I open his shirt and expose his body to the light. For a moment, I hold my breath in wonder.

Perhaps he really is the Angel Raphael in human form. His precious, vulnerable body. Where the sun has not kissed him, he is pure white. Skin so white it almost glows, like warm alabaster. I trace my fingers over his belly, and the darker hair that forms a line from his navel downwards. I can hardly stop myself sliding my fingers beneath his waistband, hardly believe that I can afford to luxuriate in my anticipation. In the cool air, he is stippled with tiny goose bumps. I smooth a light touch over his belly, and his skin responds with a shiver.

It's not the body of a young man, his skin is not taut, his muscles not toned, but to me he is more beautiful for that. It is the body of a man who has lived, who has worked, who has denied himself for others. A man who has weathered what life has sent him. It is a private body, not to be seen by others, and I am well aware of my privilege. I have been staring at him for some moments and he is looking at me doubtfully, as if I might change my mind. I feel tears pricking in my eyes, then a slow smile returns to my lips.

"You're just like an angel," I whisper.

He laughs and tries to pull me to him, but I sit back straight, just out of his reach. I meet his eye so he knows the significance of what I am about to do. Slowly I open the dressing gown and let it fall from my shoulders. I let him see me, my heavy breasts, nipples hard from wanting him. I take his hand and guide it over my body, over my flat belly. I see his eyes widen as he takes me in, and the effort it takes him to drag his gaze back to my face makes me laugh. He is transfixed by me and I am elated. More than my body, I let him see me. Perhaps it is the first time I have ever let a man really see me. I am here, more present than I have ever been. This, this is how I will live the rest of my life.

He exhales and I realise that he is shaking. I slide my hand up the length of his chest and kiss him again, breathing in his breath, moving my body against his, slowly at first because we have all the time in the world to discover each other. This is completion. We do not need to speak; skin-to-skin, the most powerful silent contract.

Acknowledgements

Heartfelt gratitude to my first readers, Jo, Yasmin, Claire, Elinor and my parents, Jenny and Joe, to Sam and Jude for their encouragement, guidance and wise advice, and the whole wonderful team at Pinter & Martin (Martin, Maria, Zoë, Zoë, Emily and editors Claire and Emma). Love and thanks to my children, Cara and Sylvie, my husband, Chris, and to my much-missed friends in Ethiopia: Heran (an inspiration in so many ways), Anna, Dawit, Mulu, Tenaye, Redeat and to "Teddy", wherever he is.

The story "The Donkeys and the Hyenas" is an Ethiopian folk tale collected by Elizabeth Laird in her lovely book, *The Lure of the Honey Bird: the story tellers of Ethiopia* (Birlinn Ltd, 2013).